RED

THE COLOR OF
MURDER

Jane Pecora

ISBN 978-1-64471-944-2 (Paperback)
ISBN 978-1-64471-945-9 (Digital)

Copyright © 2019 Jane Pecora
All rights reserved
First Edition

All rights reserved. No part of this publication may be reproduced, distributed, or transmitted in any form or by any means, including photocopying, recording, or other electronic or mechanical methods without the prior written permission of the publisher. For permission requests, solicit the publisher via the address below.

Covenant Books, Inc.
11661 Hwy 707
Murrells Inlet, SC 29576
www.covenantbooks.com

Thank you to Susan Studier, author of "Tainted Rye Crisp," who said, "Jane, you have written a best seller," giving me my first words of encouragement.

Thank you to Denise and Shannon Hein because I would not have attempted to publish this book without their excitement and financial aid.

Thank you to Sheila Jarrett, editor at the Williams S. Hein Co., Denver satellite, for the initial editing and formatting.

Thank you to Winter Hein who said, "It's still to date, one of the best things I have read."

Chapter 1
Where Did the Sunshine Go?

Monday, September 2, Early Morning

As I sat on the cold hard concrete floor of a small cell, I stared up at the bar-covered window, wondering how I ended up here. I felt physically exhausted, and if I had any emotions at all, they were completely suppressed.

"I'm in jail?" I whispered hoarsely, questioning reality. I think I heard someone say I would die here. Who would say that? I did feel like I wanted to die. My spirit was so tired—too tired to try to live another day. I tried to recall the events of the past few days and had no remembrance of them whatsoever.

"Come on, Jo. Think." My brain hurt as I tried to bring reason to my situation. I could see I was wearing a short-sleeved white V-neck scrub uniform. "How on earth did I get this horrible thing on?" I asked myself. I wondered if it had numbers printed across the back of it.

The sun was streaming in, and I felt the shadow of the black bars on my body. I loved the sunshine. It usually made me smile, but not today. I was barely comforted by the slight warmth from the light. I tried to smile to see if I could lift my spirit, but my face was contrary—frozen in a hard, blank frowning daze. As the sun slowly rose higher, I knew before long, the streams of light would disappear and not return again until tomorrow morning's dawn.

"Have I been here longer than a morning?" I wondered. "Let me think now. I worked last week at Salet's Department Store. I worked on Friday to closing and was looking forward to my first Saturday off in a month. I went right home. I wrote a letter to Robert, and I went to bed. And…and…and then what?" I asked myself.

"Shiny." I thought I heard Dad's voice whispering to me. He often called me Shiny when he was in a playful mood.

"Sheeny, Shiny," my older siblings teased me, mocking Dad's nickname for me. They said it was because I had a greasy bald head. I didn't feel very shiny. I felt my hair. It felt pretty greasy.

"Don't leave me, sunshine," I cried out to the last rays of light as they disappeared on the floor. I rested my head back on the cream-painted steel door of this small, barren space and shut my eyes. I couldn't remember the present, so my mind wandered to the past, drifting to a sunshiny summer day of a long time ago.

Chapter 2

The Red Lips

I lived in a small farming community where corn and cows are the main decoration of the countryside. The summers are hot and the winters are cold there in Havana, Minnesota, in the United States of America, the land of the free and the home of the brave.

I do not know how our town got its name, Havana. There were no Cubans living there, as you might think. It was just like most of Southeastern Minnesota. The majority of the population were Norwegians and Germans who had rushed into the area, grabbing land grants after the 1851 Treaty of Traverse des Sioux, an unjust pact that pushed the natives out of the area.

I was five years old. I was neither brave nor free. I was afraid of the dark and a host of other things, and I belonged to her. She scared me too. At this young and tender age, I did not perceive that anything was wrong with her.

I stood next to her in the bathroom of the big house, watching her put on her bright red lipstick. I always referred to it as the "big house" because we moved into it after having lived with Grandmother Lewis in a house that was half the size. With my hands on the edge of the sink, I was just tall enough so my chin could rest there too if I stood on my tiptoes.

She adjusted her new black glasses. The large cat eyes had rhinestones embedded in the edges. They were bold and modern, just like her personality. She opened up a new tube of lipstick, twisted up the waxy emollient, and leaned into the mirror to paint those lips her favorite color—bright red. She rubbed her lips together, evening out the color. As she stepped back from the sink, she pushed the sides of her dark brown hair back away from her face. Smiling, she sent herself an imaginary kiss into the mirror. Her blue eyes were twinkling as she looked at herself. I think she liked what she saw. I never saw her look at me that way.

She…was my mother. I followed her into the kitchen where she brewed herself a cup of tea and sat down at the table. I watched her first blow away the hot steam and then take a sip with those painted lips that left behind a red smear on the edge of the cup.

I don't know what got into me, but I had the urge to sit on her lap. I simply could not remember ever sitting on her lap. I saw her hold my baby brother, Jimmy, on her lap to feed him. I wondered what it would be like to be hugged by her. I saw her hug Dad sometimes. I got as close to her as I could without touching her and stared up at her. She ignored me. She put the cup of hot tea down and relaxed back on the chair. That was my moment. My little hands grabbed her dress for support, and I hopped up on her knees as fast as I could, all the while looking up at her face. She reacted with surprise and was greatly irritated. Her hands grabbed me and shoved me down onto the floor.

"What do you think you are doing? Get off me. You are way too big for that." Her voice was angry and scolding, as if I had hurt her.

Way too big? I put the question to my inner thoughts. Just this week, Jimmy and I were in Dr. Androvich's office for a checkup. Hadn't the doctor just told her I was quite small for my age, below average on the growth and weight charts? He said it as if I was not normal or something. In fact, he was quite surprised at the smallness of my size, remembering what a chubby newborn baby I had been.

*****

"Make sure she drinks milk every day," ordered Dr. Androvich, looking at Mother with a big smile. He had his hand on her back. I hate it when he touches me.

"Milk? Ick," I responded.

"Milk!" said Dr. Androvich, looking directly at me with a snarl.

Mother jerked me down off the examining table and snapped me on the top of my head. "Certainly," she said, smiling with her face ever so close to Dr. Androvich's face.

Yuck, I thought. *If Mother wasn't standing between us, I would kick him in the shins.*

When he examined Jimmy, his tone was quite different. He was so proud of how big Jimmy was and so "healthy-looking" with "such strong little legs." Jimmy was two now, but he had yet to say a word.

I shuddered at the memory of Dr. Androvich. Mother was always laughing with him while he held and patted her hand.

*****

"Look what your grubby little hands did to my dress," she continued to debase me. I instinctively turned my palms up to see if they were "grubby." I didn't mean to hurt her, but she hurt me. I had no physical pain, but my insides felt the bruising of my affection.

Her face had that grimacing look that told me what was coming next. At the moment she reached out to slap me, there was a quick triple knock on the screen door.

"Hello, Sandy?" Mrs. Bjornevik called in through the screen, sounding bright and perky. She was coming over from across the street for coffee. I was saved.

Mother recoiled, and in an instant, the contorted face turned into a cheery, albeit fake, smile.

"Come in, Henrietta, the coffee's hot," she said with phony delight. Teatime in the afternoon was a part of Mother's schedule. She was so proud of being English. She resented having to make coffee for the "immigrants" who were not civilized enough to appreciate the value of tea.

I leaped up and hastily backed away out of the reach of Mother. I have always called her *Mother*. *Mom* was too casual. She was never casual. Her speech was formal from the intelligence that was behind it. *Mama* was too babyish. She expected grown-up behavior from a two-year-old. And *Mommy* was just too warm. Her true persona behind the facade of super niceties was cold as ice.

I stayed in the room but behind Mother, waiting for Henrietta to notice me. Mother told me to call her Mrs. Bjornevik, but I loved her first name. She was a Norwegian.

With ridicule, Mother had said, "The Norvee'gins"—saying it with a strong accent on the "vee"— "only came to my country to profit from the free land of the Homestead Act. They are all a bunch of freeloaders."

Mother could trace her lineage from the first white settlers in Virginia to England and there back to AD 1612, from the family of Tredegar Morgan, follower of Queen Elizabeth I, who was quite possibly a relative of the queen. Imagine that. I have never cared where I came from. I just care where I am going.

I knew I liked Norwegians, even if Mother did not care for them. I lingered at the foot of the stairs in case I needed to make a quick exit. In she walked, Henrietta Bjornevik, practically dancing, as if she could not contain the joy within. I wondered what made her seem so happy all the time. I liked it. She was tall and chubby with rosy cheeks, and she oozed something I knew I greatly desired but wasn't sure what. Her thick hair was blond and very long but always braided, with the braids neatly wrapped around her head.

Just like a halo, I pondered. I loved her homemade dress, which was colored the lightest of blues, silky-looking, and beautifully sewn. The full skirt of it flowed around her legs. I wondered what an angel looked like. I figured just like Henrietta.

"Henrietta." I thought I had whispered her name. I loved saying it because it had four syllables. My own name was just one short syllable—Jo.

Henrietta looked around to see where the little whisper came from. She didn't disappoint me.

"Jo? There you are. Come here, love. I need a great big hug from a tiny little girl."

Slowly, I moved toward Henrietta. My heart wanted to run to her, but my mind said, *Tread lightly. Mother is watching.* I glanced a peek at Mother who was so in control of herself in front of guests. Her face showed that fake smile, her shoulders back and her chin up. She would say she was "proper." I would say she was proud.

The Bible says, "Pride goes before destruction, and a haughty spirit before a fall."[1]

"Come on then, Jo," Henrietta encouraged me, squatting down on her heels to meet me eye level. That was all I needed. I ran right into those inviting and outstretched arms. She was soft and warm and tender and oh so cuddly and smelled so good. I melted into her embrace and felt her love surround me. Yes, I liked it. When she gently released me, I looked at her face as I stepped back. She was smiling, and her eyes were twinkling. I could actually feel peace from her to me, pouring into my soul. Peace that passes all understanding was something I had remembered from church. Mother dislikes church.

"Thank you, love. I needed that," she said to me out loud. I said it back to her with my eyes, but my lips were silent. "You are very beautiful," Henrietta said, patting my dark blond hair. With her encouragement, a smile came over my face, and I ran outside to play in the sunshine. Usually, the farther away from Mother, the better.

Henrietta did not have any children. Mother said she was barren and unfulfilled. I did not know what barren meant, but Mother made it sound like a bad word. I did not understand the unfulfilled part either. I thought it might mean hungry, but Mother said Henrietta was fat from eating too much. Mother never said anything nice about fat people. I tried hard to remember if she said anything nice about anyone.

My sister, Jessie, and brother, Johnny, were in the sand box making roads and mountains. Jessie was eight, and Johnny was seven. They were like two peas in a pod. Upon first meeting, most people thought they were twins. They were always together, snickering and whispering. I skipped over to them, feeling happy, but before I could touch the pile of sand, Jessie let out a disgusted sigh.

"Arrrh," she growled like a dog. "Don't touch our stuff, Jo. You will wreck it."

"I want to help," I said.

---

[1] Proverbs 16:18 (NKJV)

Jessie stood up and put her hands on her hips, a gesture she inherited from Mother. She took a menacing step toward me. She only thought of me as an intruder or an irritant.

"We don't want your help," she said firmly, emphasizing the "we." She always spoke for Johnny. She was a mini Mother. God knows I didn't want two mothers. Johnny looked up at me with a smile but remained silent. He merely did whatever Jessie told him to do. He lived for her approval. I never understood why.

I backed down and sauntered over to the swing set, wondering where that feeling of peace went. I loved to swing. I tried to get as high as I could, thinking I could get closer to God or at least an angel.

Maybe my foot can touch the edge of heaven, I thought.

After an hour or so, Henrietta came out of the house. She crossed the yard and went back to her own house across the street. I watched her every step of the way. She paused at the beautiful flower garden in front of her house and picked a white daisy. She put it in her hair. There were no flowers in my yard. As she put her hand on the doorknob, she turned and gave me a wave.

Yes, I thought. *That is what an angel looks like.*

CHAPTER 3
DRAB AND DREARY

Monday, September 2, Noon

A blat from a loudspeaker brought me back to the moment.

"Step away from the door," a piercing command came over the loudspeaker. I jumped up in instant obedience for fear of the unknown.

The door of my cell opened, and another command came.

"Step out, and step into the line!" Women of all ages and color stepped into the line. I saw the numbers on the backs of their uniforms. Well, that answered one of my questions.

I wonder what my number is? I thought to myself.

Then I heard, "#05135775! Step into the line!"

I stood frozen like a dumb sheep without understanding. I didn't know what was going on.

"#05135775! Step into the line!" The command was repeated.

Then #11284774, reaching out and taking a brave step into my cell, took pity on me and pulled me into the line behind #24656776.

"That's your number, Dumbo," she whispered hoarsely to me. "You can thank me later. I just saved you from a beating."

"Where are we going?" I whispered back.

"To the Starlight Room, for dinner and dancing, you idiot." She shoved me forward.

"No talking!" blared the loudspeaker again. I followed the line down the corridor of cells and into the cafeteria. I did whatever the woman in front of me did.

I have a very sensitive sense of smell, and my nose was telling me whatever we were eating was indiscernable. I picked up a tray and slid it along the edge of the counter as kitchen workers filled it with a napkin, plastic spoon, cup of Kool-Aid, and plate. Then three plops of food. The first plop was white. Potato was my guess. The second plop was brown. Meat was my guess. The third plop was orange. No guessing there. I smelled the squash as the plop hit the plate.

As I followed #24656776 to our specific table, the stench of the squash caused my mind to wander again to another day when I was just a small child.

Chapter 4
The Red Dress

My thoughts drifted to Mother. I never think about her this much. I couldn't help but think about one of her dinners. She was religious about routine, hating any deviation from it. Mealtimes were never late. Breakfast at eight, dinner at noon, and supper at six.

Outside in the sunshine, I was swinging as high as I could get. I kept looking to the west, knowing soon, I would see the big green car coming around the corner, bringing Dad home from work. Dad was very proud of his car. It was a 1952 Ford Greenbrier Mainline Tudor Sedan. He said Joe Louis, the heavyweight champion of the world, worked in the Ford factory, and maybe he even helped put together this very car. I thought that was an awfully long name for a car. Dad loved saying it. It was three years old already and still looked brand-new.

Mother hated the color of it. Almost every time she opened the door of the car, she would wrinkle up her nose and say through clenched teeth, "I hate green." Dad would ignore her.

One time, she said, "Dr. Androvich drives a red car, and the top comes down." Dad did not ignore this comment. It was a Sunday afternoon, and we were all going to Rochester for ice cream. Dad got out the car, ran over to Mother's side, opened the door, pulled her out, and shut the door. He got back in the car and left her standing in the driveway. Dad seemed angry, so Jessie, Johnny, and I remained silent. Only Jimmy dared to babble his baby talk all the way to the Tastee Freeze.

Dad had an explosive personality. I noticed it more and more the older I got. Fortunately, most of his anger was directed at Mother and not me.

Through the screen door, I heard the wall clock chime six times, and immediately, the car was in sight. Mother stepped out onto the porch and smoothed her new dress down from her large bosom and over her narrow hips, turning from side to side. I was intrigued because people said she was quite beautiful. I didn't see it.

"Store-bought," she had proudly called the dress. It was an A-line red cotton sundress with wide shoulder straps. It was just long enough to cover her kneecaps. The white top stitching set off the big white buttons that went down the front, bringing your eyes to the new white leather sandals.

Jessie and Johnny leaped out of the sandbox and dashed inside, not wanting to incur Mother's wrath. She followed them in. I waited until Dad got out the car and called to me.

"Jo, let's go," said Dad. I jumped off the swing and met him at the steps to the house. He pantomimed a little boxing. I boxed him back as hard as I could, but it only made him laugh.

Dad loved the sport of boxing. He was a Golden Gloves champion boxer when he was in the Navy. He kept his worn-out red leather boxing gloves tied together on a hook in the entry. There was an extra pair there too for whatever opponent dared to challenge him. His red and gold silk boxing robe hung on a hook in his closet upstairs. It intrigued me, and I remember sneaking in there once to feel it. I never did see him wear it, so I just imagined Dad wearing it, dancing around the boxing ring, jabbing his fists in the air.

"Time to eat," he said as we went through the door together. He knew dinner would be on the table as soon as he stepped inside the house. It always was. I dreaded dinnertime. It meant a glass of disgusting milk. I didn't like many foods. I liked bread and butter, and that's about it.

Mother insisted everyone sit in the same chair at every meal. The table was round. Dad sat closest to the door. I sat to the right of Dad—a place that made me feel safe. Johnny sat on the other side of me. Jessie was next to Johnny. Mother was next to Jessie, and the baby, Jimmy, with his jet-black hair, sat in his high chair, right in between Mother and Dad.

As the food was being served, Mother said in a very chipper voice, "Here, Jo, have some squash." She was reaching the dish across the table to me, noting I did not take any on the pass around.

"No, thank you. I don't like squash," I said. I took the dish from her and passed it to the right. Johnny took it and set it down. I knew that she knew that I didn't like it.

"Just taste it," said Mother. "You will love it. It is fresh from the garden. It is so delicious." Mother loved her vegetable garden. There were no weeds in it, but there were no flowers in it either. I made a mental note that when I grow up, I will only have flowers in my garden, just like Henrietta.

"I don't want any," I repeated loudly. *She must be deaf,* I thought. I didn't care if it was fresh from the garden or old from the can. Squash was squash, and no matter how you fixed it, it was revolting.

"Take a bite, and you will like it," said Mother, smiling that plastic smile as she put a huge plop of it on my plate, again reaching across the table and breaking one of her own table rules to do it. That plastic smile was a good mask for the contorted sneer that was under it. It fooled most people, but it never fooled me.

"That's way too much," I pleaded.

I knew I didn't like squash. I didn't like the color of it. I didn't like the smell of it. I didn't like the texture of it. I knew I hated it. She knows I hate it. I took my fork and pushed it to the edge of my plate so it wouldn't contaminate the rest of the food. I looked around the table. Jessie and Johnny were eating theirs. Dad was even taking more. I wondered if his taste buds were broken.

Pretty soon, Dad, Jessie, and Johnny were done eating all their food, including their squash. I was amazed. None of them had complained once. Jessie and Johnny asked permission to leave the table and headed toward the other room to play cards with Dad. At the doorway, Jessie turned around and looked back at me. She snickered and whispered something to Johnny. With taunting grins, they both stuck their tongues out at me. That stung, and I had to just sit there and take it.

"I'm done too," I exclaimed with authority, thinking I could convince Mother to let me down from the table.

"Oh no, you are not." Her voice grated on my tiny nerves. All my food was gone except for the squash. That should count for something. "Jo, when you eat your squash, you can come into the other room and play cards with the rest of the family," said Mother as she washed Jimmy's face and hands.

"I can't eat it," I whined, as if I was already queasy. "It will make me sick. I'm just going to sit here till I die."

"Oh, don't be so dramatic," snapped Mother as she pulled Jimmy from his high chair and carried him into the other room.

Poor, little Jo, I thought to myself as I sat there all alone in the kitchen. Jimmy didn't have to eat all his squash. He just smeared it all over his high chair. "Yeah, I know. He's just a baby," I said it mockingly to myself. He looked to me like he was big enough to be forced into eating his squash. I felt very sad listening to all the family laughing and playing in the other room. I wanted to play cards with Dad too.

I pushed the squash to the other side of my plate, thinking somehow I could make it disappear. Then, all of a sudden, a great idea popped into my head. I glanced at the doorway to make sure no one could see me. I picked up my plate and scraped all the squash onto the table and set the plate right back down on top of it. I felt my face break into a smile of relief as I thought, *Yes, this is a good idea. Squash all gone.*

"Mother, I'm done!" I hollered into the next room.

Mother came in, looked at my plate, and said, "Really, you ate it?" I could tell she was very surprised.

Tentatively, I nodded my head yes. Now, in her presence, I was not so sure of myself.

"See, that didn't taste so bad," she said. "Did it?"

I was not prepared for the question, but I was resolved to get down from the table. Tentatively, I shook my head no.

"All right then, come into the other room, and play cards," she declared my liberation.

It worked, I thought. Smiling with relief, I jumped down and scurried to the next room. She followed me in.

After some time had passed, Mother got up and went into the kitchen to wash the dishes. As I saw her go in, a funny feeling crept into my stomach.

Uh-oh, I thought to myself. *This is not a good feeling.* Then what I feared in the back of my mind happened.

Mother cried out to me from the kitchen in that witchlike voice. Her shrieking utterance caused the funny feeling in my stomach to turn into a real sick feeling. Nothing imagined here.

"Jo! What did you do? You are very bad! Come in here this instant."

All play immediately stopped, and all eyes bored through me like daggers of fire. I could read the eyes. "Guilty!" they said.

Slowly, I got up as Dad, Jessie, Johnny, and baby Jimmy all watched me in silence, wondering just what "naughty" Jo had done now.

As I slowly entered the kitchen with my head hanging down, my worst fears were laid bare. There stood Mother, holding my plate with the cold squash, now doubly nauseating, scraped back onto it.

"You are very naughty indeed," Mother scolded. "Get back in your chair right now. You are going to eat your squash."

I refused to cry, but the tears were leaking out of my eyes anyway as I climbed back onto my chair where I always sat so righteously next to Dad. He was not there now, unable to protect me from her. I strained to hear what was going on in the other room. The house was silent. I know they were straining to hear what was going on in the kitchen.

Mother scooped up a big spoonful of cold, vile, nasty squash and squeezed open my mouth. I tried to hold it shut, but the pain from the pressure of her long fingernails pressing into my cheeks was severe. She callously stuffed in the squash. The force of the spoon on my baby teeth hurt me. I tried to swallow. I just couldn't do it. I was choking. In that moment, I knew I was going to die of squash poisoning. Regrettably, my gag reflex kicked in, and I couldn't control what would happen next. Up it came—the cold, slimy squash—

along with the rest of my dinner, spewed out all over the table, all over her, and all over myself.

"My dress!" Mother screamed. I looked at her new red "store-bought" dress. It was definitely spattered with the contents of my stomach. "You little brat."

Brat? How I could be the brat? What about her? She was the one shoving poison down my throat.

"Don't you move!" she growled. She ran to the sink and desperately washed off the vomit. Then she patted herself dry with a fresh towel.

I was hoping she was cooling down, but as she turned toward me again, I could see it was just the opposite. She was heating up. If she was mad before, she was furious now. She grabbed me by the arm and pulled me off my chair.

"Dad!" I cried out uselessly. It was still silent in the other room, and he did not come to save me. She spanked me. Again and again, her hand slapped my bare legs until they were left stinging and red.

"Now go get your pajamas on, Jo, and get right into bed. You are very naughty!" she roared as she shoved me toward the stairs.

"No, I'm not naughty. Henrietta says I am very beautiful. You are naughty!" I screamed it to her through the sobbing. That was a mistake. Mother grabbed me back.

"You little monster!" she growled. "Don't ever speak to me that way again." She delivered three more fresh slaps to my still stinging legs and shoved me once again toward the stairs. "You get out of here right now."

Straightening up and throwing her shoulders back, Sandra marched pompously into the living room. She sat down on the couch and pulled her big King James Bible out from the shelf under the coffee table. She paged through the leaves until she reached the book of Proverbs. She stopped at chapter 13 and read aloud verse 24: "He that spareth his rod hateth his son: but he that loveth him chasteneth him betimes."[2]

---

[2] Proverbs 13:24 (KJV)

As I turned on the light in the stairwell, I wondered if *betimes* meant the same as *bedtimes*. Then slowly, and with trepidation, I ventured up the stairs. This was almost the worst part of the punishment. I was afraid of the dark, and I was afraid of the upstairs even if it wasn't dark when I was alone. Usually, when it was time for me to go to bed, baby Jimmy was already up there in his crib. I could manage the fear if he was there even though he was only two years old. About halfway up the stairs, I could hear the others beginning to play again.

That's right. The show's over, folks, I thought, feeling hate for them all. I know, big thoughts for such a little girl.

Once in the bathroom, I climbed up on the toilet to reach a washrag in the cupboard above it. I washed my face, stripped off the puke-laden clothes, and shoved them in the hamper. I found my well-worn nightgown on one of the three hooks on the back of the bathroom door, right where I had hung it that morning after I got dressed for the day. That night, I gladly brushed my baby teeth and rinsed the lingering taste of bile out of my mouth.

I sat down on the floor and pulled one of my feet up to see the bottom of it. We ran barefoot all summer long, and Mother always insisted we wash our feet before getting into bed. Yep, just as I suspected, it was very dirty. Just to punish her, I decided I would not wash them this night. I snapped the bathroom light off and ran as fast as I could across the hall. I leaped quickly into my bed, pulling my feet safely in under the covers and out of the reach of the boogeyman, whom I suspected lived under there.

Now safe in my bed, I said to no one in particular, "When I grow up, I will never make my little children eat squash. Then they will never have to be naughty." It was a promise to myself.

Dad had taught me to say prayers before I went to sleep. It was supposed to go like this: "Dear, Jesus, bless Mother, Dad, Jessie, Johnny, Jo, and baby Jimmy. Make me a good girl and forgive all my sins. In Jesus's name. Amen."

This night, I folded my hands and said, "Dear, Jesus, I wish Henrietta could be my mother." I wondered if angels could be mothers. "Make me a good girl, but don't forgive Mother. She is the one who is naughty. In Jesus's name. Amen." It was comforting to pray.

It was twilight now, neither dark nor light. The sun was out of sight, and the full moon glowed right through the window and onto my tear-streaked face. Thankfully, I fell asleep.

Chapter 5
I Can't Remember

Monday, September 2, After Lunch

"Stand up, and return your trays!" I was jolted to reality by the blaring loudspeaker. I looked at my tray. In my meditation, I had stirred all the food together, creating a swirly muck. I had eaten nothing. Obediently, I stood and picked up my tray.

"You'll eat it when you are hungry enough," chuckled #112842774. Her plate was completely empty.

Stepping into the line behind #2465776, I did whatever she did to dispose of the tray and its contents. We were marched back to our cells where, after stepping inside, the door slammed shut. I was numb. The cell was bleak. I laid down on the narrow cot, feeling despondent and weary. It wasn't long before I heard footsteps coming down the corridor. I wondered who would get a visitor. As the sound got closer, the steps slowed and stopped at my door. I sat up as the door unlocked. In stepped a very professionally dressed woman. She looked harmless. Maybe because she was just ordinary looking.

"Jo Lewis?" she asked.

"I was named after a professional boxer," I offered. Somehow, I felt I had to defend my name.

"Oh, is that so?" She smiled. "May I speak with you for a few minutes?"

"Are you a lawyer?" That was my first guess.

"No, I am a court-appointed psychiatrist. My name is Dr. Westfield," she said.

"A doctor of psychiatry, hmmm. Does someone think I am crazy?" I know I thought I was crazy, at least today anyway.

"Well, I don't know, but I would like to talk with you for a while about your case." She held up a folder that was in her hand. I noticed my number, 05135775, on the label.

"Sure," I said without emotion. "I too would like to know what my case is." I stood and pulled the lone chair out from my small table and offered it to her. Even though I couldn't remember yesterday, I did remember I had manners. Then I sat on the edge of my cot, trying to remember what could possibly be my case.

"Thank you," she commented as she sat down and opened her folder. I looked her over while she read the top paper. She would have had to go to school for a long time to become a doctor, I surmised. She could be over thirty but not much. There was no wedding ring on her hand. In fact, she wore no jewelry at all. I thought all girls wanted to be married. I know I sure did. She must be what Mother called an "old maid."

I could just hear what Mother's comment would be if she were sizing her up: "I could show her how to get a man." As if getting a man was the only important accomplishment in life.

I had never thought of a woman being a doctor either. Of course, the only doctor I knew was Dr. Androvich, and he was a bonehead.

"How are you doing?" asked Dr. Westfield.

"I honestly don't know." I knew nothing. I felt blank.

"Are you hungry?" she asked.

"No," I answered.

"I see you didn't eat your lunch." She seemed concerned.

"You know that about me already?" I was surprised.

She chuckled. "There are eyes everywhere, dear. Do you know where you are?"

"I'm guessing jail? Do not pass go? Do not collect two hundred dollars?" I said.

"You are in the Steele County Detention Center," she said.

"Oh, I've heard of that. When can I go home?" I asked.

"Can you tell me why you are here?" she asked, ignoring my question.

"No. I can't remember anything. I can't focus. My mind just wanders to the past," I said. "I can't remember yesterday or the day before. I am not really sure how many days I am missing. I don't know what day today is. I just remember I found myself sitting on the floor in this cell this morning, watching the sunshine coming in the window."

"What things in the past are you thinking about?" she asked.

"Mostly my mother, I guess," I said. "So why am I here? Please tell me. And when can I go home?" I pleaded.

"You have been arrested for murder, Jo," Dr. Westfield said it as she intently watched my face.

"Murder? Are you sure? I don't think I could hurt anyone." I was really surprised.

"Yes, I'm pretty sure," she said, tapping my file.

"I have a good memory. I can even remember the day I was born. I remember everything that has ever happened to me. I just can't remember yesterday, and I am not sure how many days before that I am missing. How could I be arrested for murder? Who was murdered?"

"Your mother," she said, looking straight into my eyes.

"My mother...?" I tried desperately to think. "She doesn't like me. I admit I don't like her. I even mostly hate her, but kill her?" Struggling to think of recent events, I whispered, "Murder. Murder. How can that be? I am just an ordinary small-town girl," I said. "There has never been a murder in my town that I know of. Nobody knows how to kill another person. Murder."

I contemplated the horror of a murder. I contemplated the horror of the murder of my mother. My head began pounding at the temples with pain, and I laid down to get some relief. I pulled my body up tight into a fetal position and began to cry.

"Dad. Where's my dad? Can I call my dad? My mother doesn't like me, but my dad does." I couldn't stop the flood of emotion, and the sobbing came from deep inside me, pouring out like a waterfall. "I don't remember how I got here, but I remember Dad on the day I was born. He named me Jo."

I kept sobbing. Something way down inside me felt a loss, and the pain seemed so real, but I just could not remember the cause of it. Dr. Westfield said she would come back later after I felt better.

Chapter 6

The Red Baby Lips

I remember the day. I was born on Saturday, May 13, 1950, to James and Allesandra Lewis. I got on my mother's bad side right away by interrupting her dinner that day. She had been in labor since early morning and was not smiling, knowing a new baby was on the way. Unfortunately for me, just as she was about to serve dinner to my dad, his mother, my sister, and my brother, a sharp and excruciating pain stabbed her in the back.

"Time to go to the hospital!" she yelled and sat down on a kitchen chair. "James, call Dr. Androvich and tell him we are on the way. Let your mother know she has to watch the kids and then get that darned car started."

That darned car was dad's first car, a Brewster Green 1931 Ford Model A Five-Window Coupe. Since it was nineteen years old already, it was not always reliable.

When the pain ebbed, Mother went to the bathroom and opened the medicine chest. She found her bright red lipstick and refreshed her lips. She was not about to be seen in public without her lipstick on. Under the sink, waiting for this day, was her small and already packed bag. Bending even slightly to pick it up caused her pain, and she groaned loudly as she grabbed it. She unzipped the side pocket and slid in the tube of red lipstick.

Grandmother Lewis came out of her back bedroom after James rapped on her door.

"Mom, come out, and be with the kids!" he yelled. "Sandra is ready to go to the hospital."

Grandmother Lewis was Sandra's public enemy number one. When James had announced he was going to marry Allesandra Burnham, she had actually fainted.

"The Burnham family!" said Grandmother Lewis. "Why, I don't believe they go to church. The women are haughty and brazen, even though they come from poverty. The men are boozers."

She had referred to Sandra as a hussy and had tried to get James to dump her, complaining she was not the proper wife for the son of a reverend. When he stood firm, she fasted and cried for three days, all to no avail.

"Dinner is ready to be served," Sandra said to Grandmother Lewis, handing her a list of directions. "I've written down all you need to know, not that you'll pay attention of any of it but just try. Okay?" Instantly, she was stricken with another stabbing pain and doubled over. "I want this over with!" she screamed out when the pain ebbed again.

Grandmother Lewis did not act sympathetic toward her pain or offended by the comment, but she was offended Sandra was pregnant again.

"If you had only used birth control properly, my dear, you wouldn't have to be going through this again," she rudely commented. She took the list from Sandra and, without looking at it, stuffed it into her pocket.

"Oh, for crying out loud," said Sandra. Sandra rolled her eyes and waddled out to the waiting car. "Proverbs 27:15!" she yelled out the quote. "'A continual dropping on a very rainy day and a contentious woman are alike.'[3] You would know that if you read your Bible." Under her breath, she muttered, "God, I hate that woman."

My grandmother, Clara Lewis, lived with us. Or, rather, we lived with her. It was obvious to anyone around she and my mother constantly irritated each other with snide remarks. She irritated me too. She seemed to have only two grandchildren. She pampered Jessie and Johnny. Jimmy and I were invisible to her.

---

[3] Proverbs 27:15 (KJV)

"One of each is all you need," she said it often enough and always seemed to be looking at me when she said it. When she looked at Jimmy, she would comment, "Jet-black hair. I wonder where that came from?"

After her husband, the Rev. Cedric Hamilton Lewis, pastor of the Owatonna Presbyterian Church, passed in 1941, she gave his Brewster Green 1931 Ford Model A Five-Window Coupe to her only son, James Barrington Lewis, my father. He had just turned fifteen years old, and the pain of losing his father was diminished by the joy of receiving the car. After all, what fifteen-year old boy wouldn't just love to have his own car? Clara knew next to nothing about cars or the laws about them, so James took full advantage of it, driving everywhere without a license and giving himself a new sense of independence.

Dad loved to speed. He bragged he could get his Model A, which was only made to go up to sixty-five miles per hour, up to speeds over eighty miles per hour on the newly tarred road out in the country. Tonight was a night he thought he had a good excuse to legally speed, and he did. He made the five-and-eight-tenths-mile trip to the hospital in just five minutes.

Things went fast as soon as they arrived at the hospital. Sandra knew the routine and had delayed going to the hospital for as long as she could, knowing upon arrival there, she would be confined to the bed. I was more than ready to come out and see the world. Dad and Mother parted ways once inside. Mother was checked and taken immediately to the delivery room as she was already wanting to push.

"Dr. Androvich, report to labor and delivery," was heard over the hospital loudspeaker. "Dr. Androvich."

"Dr. Androvich," said Dad, repeating the loudspeaker. He shook his head. "There is something about him I just don't like. Maybe 'cause Sandra thinks he is some kind of god."

Dad stepped into the waiting room where he found a radio. He turned it on and tuned in to NBC. To his, delight the radio announcer was discussing his favorite sport, boxing.

"Did you know Joe Louis was born on this day, May 13, thirty-six years ago?" asked the first radio announcer.

"No, I did not," responded the second announcer.

"Well, how about that," said Dad.

"Yes, that's right, and that is why tonight, we are replaying the sports broadcast of the world-famous rematch of the heavyweight boxing championship from June 22, 1938, with Joe Louis and his contender, Max Schmeling," said the first radio announcer.

James couldn't believe his good fortune. Now this was exciting. He did not bother to sit, knowing the fight would be over all to soon—exactly two minutes and four seconds, as he recalled it.

Instantly, the voice of the ring announcer was heard. "Here we are at the packed Yankee Stadium..." And the fight was on between Maximillian Schmeling and Joe Louis, the Detroit Brown Bomber and heavyweight champion of the world. Dad punched his fists together like he was testing his boxing gloves.

Through the radio, the deafening roar of the crowd could be heard, and one could feel they were crazy with anticipation. James was so excited that, for the next few moments, he forgot where he was and why he was there. He couldn't believe his good fortune. He remembered being only twelve years old and listening to this same fight twelve years earlier. He was taken back in time, remembering he had stood as close to the radio as he could get in his friend's house with great anticipation of the fight because his own self-righteous mother would not allow such nonsense to be played on her radio.

Again, the voice of the ring announcer grabbed his attention. "Joe Louis is in his corner now, prancing and jumping..."

James reached out and turned the volume on the radio up. He began prancing around the small waiting room, throwing a few punches to the left and to the right, listening intently.

The announcer continued. "Schmeling is losing steam..."

And the was fight was over—a TKO for Joe Louis, beating Maximillian Schmeling in less than one round of fast and furious boxing. James leaped up and cheered for Joe Louis. Then he thought about where he really was. Smiling and jubilant, he sat down in the waiting room chair to wait for more good news. It wasn't long before a nurse came out to get him.

"Mr. Lewis," said the smiling nurse.

"Yes?" said James with anticipation as he jumped up out of his chair.

"It's a girl," she announced. "Mother and baby girl are doing just fine. You can go in and see Sandra now, and I'll bring in the baby."

"It's a girl? Where are they?" James was excited.

"Just down this hall and on the left—room number 204," informed the nurse.

"Thank you," said James over his shoulder as he rushed off to see Sandra. Once in the room, James saw Sandra still wasn't smiling.

"Good work, doll," he said to Sandra as he bent to kiss her freshly painted red lips. She did not pucker up but let him give her the dutiful peck. "How do you feel?" he asked.

"Ugly and sore," said Sandra, rubbing her distended belly. "This one is so big she really ruined me, inside and out."

"Oh, what do you mean?" questioned James.

"I'll never get my shape back. No more kids. Do you hear me?"

"I hear you." He was beginning to feel a little deflated.

"I don't think you do." She was adamant.

"Mr. Lewis." The nurse appeared at the doorway and walked into the room, heading straight for James. In her arms was a tiny bundle wrapped in a pink cotton receiving blanket. "I will give her to you since your wife does not want to hold her yet." She smiled broadly, noticing the touch of red lipstick on his lips. *He sure is a handsome guy*, she thought.

James glanced at Sandra who was looking away from him and out of the window. He was overcome with excitement and was a bit unsure why Sandra was so melancholy. He held out his arms to take the baby.

"She is a heavyweight, that's for sure," continued the nurse. "I just weighed her in at nine pounds and ten ounces." With that comment, she placed the bundled up and sleeping baby into the arms of her dad. James stared at her beautiful round face. He recalled the faces of his two other newborn children. Their heads had been misshapen and their faces bruised. There was not a mark on this one.

"Her face is so perfect," he said to the nurse.

"That's because she was breech," said the nurse proudly. "Dr. Androvich had no trouble with the delivery at all because her little bottom end was nice and fat. Enjoy," she said as she left the room.

James was instantly in love with this precious gift from God. All the world and everything in it faded from his sight. In that moment, he only saw her. He sat in the chair next to the hospital bed where Sandra lay, ignoring him. His forefinger gently circled the round face and then the outline of her tiny lips. He lifted the baby to his face and kissed her tiny lips, passing the bright red decoration on to her.

"Your lips are just like your mommy's," he said softly, and realizing where those red lips came from, he wiped his mouth on his sleeve. Then he wiped the baby's lips on the corner of her blanket. He glanced up at his apparently unhappy wife. She still ignored him. He gently unwrapped the pink blanket to look at his baby's little feet and legs.

"Wow," he said. "She is not very long, but she is indeed chubby everywhere. Look at those fat little legs." He played with her hands and feet, and slowly, she opened her great big blue eyes. She looked up at her dad and smiled. "Well, hello there, my little heavyweight!" exclaimed James to the baby. "She smiled at me!" he exclaimed to Sandra.

"Newborns don't smile," said Sandra flatly.

"Well, this newborn smiled at me," declared James.

"That is just gas," said Sandra.

"That was a smile. She knows I am her dad," James said it with certainty, not caring what the expert on every subject thought this time. "What do you want to name her?" James asked Sandra. "We haven't had much time to talk about names."

"I don't care," said Sandra unenthusiastically.

"Yes, you do," said James in disbelief.

"I'm hungry," said Sandra, changing the subject. "I asked the nurse for a snack, and she said the dinner hour is over and the kitchen is closed."

"If you tell me what you want to name the baby, I'll go get you something to eat," said James still staring at the baby girl. He couldn't take his eyes off her.

"I don't want to name her. You name her and then you go and get me something to eat." Sandra sounded irritated now.

"Well," began James teasingly. "Today is the birthday of Joe Louis, heavyweight boxing champion of the world. Now what do you think of that?"

"Just great," said Sandra, annoyed.

"Jo Lewis," said James tenderly to his new baby girl. She began to fuss and root around, looking for something to eat. Her little hands boxed the air. "Yes, Jo Lewis," he said it again.

"Yeah, Joe Louis, so what about him?" asked Sandra.

"So that is the name of my baby girl, Jo Lewis," James declared it.

"Sounds like a boy's name to me, but I just don't care. Now go and get me something to eat," said Sandra.

"Fine. Really? You don't care?" said James in delighted disbelief.

"I said I don't care, and I don't," said Sandra, sounding depressed and irritated. "Call her Jo if you want to. I'm hungry."

"Then Jo it is," he said as he wrapped her back up tightly in the pink flannel blanket.

"Here, Sandra, you take her now. She's hungry too. You can feed her while I go get you some food." James tried to hand the baby to Sandra.

Sandra turned away to the window again and pulled the sheet up over her shoulder. "Take her to the nursery. The nurses will feed her. I am not nursing this one."

"What? You love nursing," said James, trying to encourage Sandra, thinking this must be just the temporary blues. "Have you even held her yet?"

"No," said Sandra. The baby was crying now. Sandra had nursed Jessie and Johnny for six months each, not because she believed in it but because it irritated Clara Lewis, her dreaded mother-in-law. She had not enjoyed the close communion of the baby sucking at her breasts, but she got great satisfaction out of the constant stream of protesting from Clara. "Are you going to get me something to eat or not? You are starting to get on my nerves," said Sandra coldly.

"Yes, I am," said James, finally resolved to her decision. He did not understand it, but he knew not to argue with her. That never once got him anywhere. He snuggled up his baby girl to his chest and took newly born and newly named Jo to the nursery where the nurses fought for the right to feed Jo her first bottle.

CHAPTER 7
I DIDN'T DO IT

Monday, September 2, Suppertime

When Dr. Westfield left, I cried some more. It was cathartic. I don't know how long I cried, but thinking about Dad made me feel better. My head had stopped throbbing.

"Step away from the door," came the blaring of the loudspeaker. All the doors opened at the same time. "Step into the line."

I did what I was told this time. #112842774 was right behind me and gave me a shove. I didn't have the energy to react except to just obey. "Heard you murdered your mother," whispered #112842774.

"Wow, everybody knows that but me," I whispered back.

"You've got blood on your hands, girl. You'll never get out of here," snickered #24656776 over her shoulder as quietly as she could, but I heard it loud and clear. I shuddered at the possibility of it.

Supper was a little different. Two slices of brown bread, one slice of bologna, a mustard packet, red Jell-O with fruit in it, two carrot sticks, and a cup of not so hot tea. This time, I felt the hunger, and I ate the sandwich and carrot. I kept smashing and stirring the Jell-O. I hate the color red. I picked the fruit out of it but couldn't eat the Jello. I just stirred it around, thinking about blood on my hands.

Why would I even want to murder my mother? I thought to myself. *I don't even live in her house anymore. What would be the point? Did we get in a physical fight about something?* I kept asking myself questions all the way back to my cell.

Once in my cell, I heard those footsteps again. When they stopped at my door, I knew Dr. Westfield was back. She entered my cell with two coffees. This time, I noticed her navy blue suit with a starched white shirt underneath. The skirt well covered her knees. I couldn't see why anyone, professional or not, would want to be so out of style.

Twiggy was the style of the day. She was a skinny British model with very short hair, long thin legs, and mini skirts. I copied her. I usually couldn't get my skirts short enough but then I wasn't a professional either.

*****

I started thinking of how much I loved short skirts. One time, I made a very cute blue and white polyester dress that had a fat plastic zipper all the way down the front. It was shift in style with little cap sleeves. When I sewed the last stitch and tried it on, I was ecstatic. So cute and quite short. Perfect. I intended to wear it out on a date with Robert that very night.

I think I took the fastest bath I ever had because I just couldn't wait to get into the dress and show it off. Anyway, I slipped into it and zipped it up. I sauntered over to Jessie's room to show off. She always turned up her nose at my homemade clothes. Tonight, she took a look and burst out laughing.

"Good luck with that. Mom will never let you out of the house in that. It is way too short," she said.

"Well, it won't be cute if it is any longer," I said with positivity.

I heard Robert's car door shut outside, and I knew he was here. I thought maybe I could make a run for it just in case Mother had a fit, so I ran down the sixteen stairs, flew past Mother and Dad at the dining room table, said "bye," and ran out the door. Robert was standing at the bottom of the five porch steps. He looked up at me, and I think he about fell over.

"Wow!" he said, holding out his hand to me. I walked down the stairs one at a time, feeling like a runway model.

Unfortunately, when I hit the sidewalk, the door opened, and Mother stepped out to the porch. "Jo!" she screeched. "You get right back in this house. You are not going anywhere in that short dress. You will not wear it unless you add four inches to the length. You look like an advertisement for the Hubba Bubba Club."

I looked at Robert with my most pitiful crestfallen face.

"I will wait right here while you change," he said, grinning from ear to ear. His eyes twinkled at me. "Hurry up," he said.

"Okay, Robo," I said. "I will be right back."

All right then, Mother dear, I thought. I proudly walked the runway in my mind back up to my room where I found a light burgundy tent dress. I had made this one too. It needed no zipper. From the armpits down, the lightweight cotton fabric flared out like a tent. I unzipped and stepped out of my Twiggy-style dress and pulled my second choice over my head. It was just an inch above my knees.

Jessie peeked into my room. "Ha-ha, idiot. I told you so," she said.

It didn't bother me a bit. This time, I held my head high and kept the runway walk all the way down the sixteen stairs through the dining room where I smiled at Mother and Dad and then went out of the house. At the top of the porch steps, I paused for Robert to take a good look at me. I giggled.

Hmm, easy access! is what I knew he was thinking when he raised those eyebrows at me.

*****

Dr. Westfield's hair was pulled back into a neat tight bun. She wore black shoes just like the ones Grandmother Lewis wore. Yes, I think she is, what Mother would say, a typical old maid. I didn't think there was anything wrong with being single, but to Mother, it was a disease. Old Maid was one of Mother's favorite card games too. She loved to tease the loser, but she was a poor loser if she happened to lose.

"Hello, Jo," Dr. Westfield said as she entered my small cell. "If you are feeling better, I was hoping we could talk some more. I don't know if you drink coffee or not, but I brought you one."

"Yes, thank you." I gladly took the cup. I sensed kindness coming from her, which made me feel regretful that I was looking at her critically. Dad always said, "Never judge someone unless you have walked a mile in their shoes."

"Do you have a middle name?" Dr. Westfield smiled at me.

"No need for one," I commented. "I have never worn red lipstick," I blurted out.

"What does that have to do with anything?" asked Dr. Westfield.

"I hate the color red," I stated dumbly. "We had red Jell-O for supper, and I couldn't eat it even though I was hungry."

"Can we talk about your dad?" she asked, changing the subject.

"I'm sure I did not kill anybody," I said, changing the subject. "I would like to call my dad. I am sure he will come and get me if he knows I am here."

"Do you know where your dad is?" she ventured tentatively.

"His house?" I asked.

"No, he is not there," she said.

"His office in the upstairs of his mother's house?" was my next guess.

"No, he has not been there all weekend," she responded.

"Maybe he has gone fishing," I wondered.

"Where would that be?" she asked.

"I don't know. He likes to try out every lake he can find," I said. "You know, Minnesota is the Land of Ten Thousand Lakes, and I think Dad has been fishing at a thousand of them."

"Your dad is missing." She said it with what felt like a question, or was it an accusation? I was sure it was a lie, but why tell me such a horror story.

"I told you I hate the color red, didn't I?" It felt like my brain was freezing up again. Missing? Why would he be missing? How could he be missing? "Let me out, and I will find him," I said. "Maybe he has gone fishing." I was feeling terribly upset with her. "He goes fishing all the time to get away from her."

"Get away from who?" asked Dr. Westfield.

"My mother!" I yelled.

RED

Dr. Westfield spoke calmly. "He has not answered his office phone in three days. His car is nowhere to be found. Neither his mother nor your sister, Jessie, know of his whereabouts. I even got ahold of your brother John up at the U of M. John does not know where he is. I thought maybe you might be able to help us find him. I was thinking a visit from him might spark your memory."

"He is not missing! He is fishing! I hate your stories! I must be in a dream! I just need to wake up! I told you I hate the color red! Get out, or let me out! Get out, or let me out!" I kept screaming it until she left. When the door closed, it was as if my brain closed down on the present, and I could only think about a better story.

Chapter 8
The Redtailed Monkey

Dad loved to tell me stories. I loved to listen to them over and over again, as many times as he was willing to tell them. Mother disrespectfully said it was because he couldn't read for himself, so he makes up his own stories for entertainment. I enjoyed sitting on Dad's lap when I was little, listening intently to every word. I don't remember Jessie or Johnny or even baby Jimmy being there with us. I don't know where they were, and I didn't care where they were. It was just me and my dad.

"Once upon a time," began Dad. "There was a tiny little girl with great big blue eyes. She was visiting a far away country—Uganda, a country in deepest, darkest Africa. Africa was full of wild animals. Here, the little girl was on safari with her dad. This part of Uganda is the rainforest, where it is thick with trees so tall and close together you could barely ever see the sky.

"One day," Dad said, "when the little girl was investigating the campsite, she saw a beautiful flower just beyond the boundary that her dad had told her to stay within. She couldn't resist it. She skipped to the flower and picked it. She put it up to her nose and smelled it."

I thought of Henrietta Bjornevik and her beautiful flowers.

"Sniff, sniff, went the little girl. It smelled sooooo good. Just ahead, she saw another one and skipped over to that one and picked it too. She was so happy with the flowers that she kept skipping and picking them and smelling them. When her little hand was just too full to hold another flower, the little girl decided to go back to the campsite and bring her dad the beautiful flowers. She looked around but did not see the campsite. She was surprised. Now she did not know where she was. She did not think she had gone that far."

"'Dad!' she cried out. He did not hear her. She began to walk in the direction she thought was the right way. She walked and walked. Now she was getting tired and thirsty. The sun was going down, and it was getting dark very fast. She kept walking but she was getting so scared.

"'Dad!' she cried out again. He still did not hear her. He did not even know she was gone. For a while, the little girl ran as fast as she could go. Now it was so dark that she could not even see where she was going. The jungle noises were scary. She remembered her dad had said there were lots of wild animals roaming around.

"All of a sudden, she heard a chirping noise coming close. Then, through the darkness, she saw the reflection of two big jungle cat eyes. She stopped dead in her tracks, frozen with fear. '*Grrrrrrrrrrrh,*' she heard, coming from the eyes. They were coming closer and closer, ready to pounce upon the little girl. Then she heard the chirping noise again.

"Again, the little girl screamed out, 'Dad!'

"Then *bang!* went the gun. Down went the big jungle cat, which was ready to pounce on the little girl, and there stood the dad with his smoking gun. On his shoulder sat a red-tailed monkey chirping away. The red-tailed monkey knew everything about the jungle because he had lived there his whole life. He showed the dad the way to find the little girl. The little girl flew into the arms of her dad who saved her with the help of his little friend, the red-tailed monkey. The end."

When Dad stopped talking, I began to cry. Dad laughed and asked, "What's wrong, Jo?" He was surprised at my tears.

"Daddy, don't sing such a goodah song," I sobbed.

Dad laughed some more. "Well then, Dad is going to have to buy you a red-tailed monkey."

The thought of getting a red-tailed monkey lessened my sorrow, and I wanted to hear the story all over again.

Thinking about Dad and his stories eased the pain in my head.

Chapter 9
The Tiny Red Flowers

September 2, Bedtime

"Lights out!" I heard blaring over the loudspeaker.

I had no idea what time it actually was, but I was grateful to be able to change out of the white scrub uniform and into the gray T-shirt nightshirt I found under my pillow.

"Dad!" I called out to him. "Where are you?"

As I lay down, memories of a different nightgown drifted across the movie screen of my mind.

*****

It was wintertime, and we were all home from school for Christmas break. I was eleven. Dad, Jessie, Johnny, Jimmy, and I had just finished shoveling Gramma Lewis's driveway even though she didn't drive, and we were now digging out of our own driveway. The crisp cold air felt good on my face. The sun was shining, and the snow was glistening. I loved shoveling snow. It kept me out the house. Henrietta opened her door across the street and stepped out to greet us.

"Hello, Lewis family!" she yelled out in her cheery singsongy manner. I waved to her. "I could use a little help over here when you are all done over there. With that big army of volunteers, it wouldn't take you all but a few minutes."

"Sure thing!" Dad yelled back, and Henrietta stepped back inside her house.

"Not me," growled Jessie. "She could use the exercise. She should do it herself."

"Then not me either," said Johnny who was always in agreement with Jessie.

"Well then," said Dad, grinning at me. "It looks like it's just you and me, Jo." Dad already knew I wouldn't say no to Henrietta.

"Dad," said Jimmy.

"Of course, you too, Jimmy," said Dad.

When we finished shoveling out our driveway, we three hopped over to Henrietta's and shoveled her out as fast as we could, laughing and throwing shovels of snow at each other. Henrietta watched out the window, and just as we were finishing it at her doorway, she opened up the door and invited us in for just a minute. When we stepped inside, she handed Jimmy a box lined with wax paper and filled with chocolate chip cookies fresh from the oven.

"Thank you so much, James," she said. "My back hurts today. You are a lifesaver."

"You're welcome. We were willing to do it for nothing." He patted me on the back. I silently smiled at her. "Mmmmm," said Dad, smelling Jimmy's cookies. "But I don't mind the cookies."

"Dad," said Jimmy, pulling the box back.

"And here, Jo. I made this for you for Christmas. Sorry, it is not wrapped, but I am out of wrapping paper, and I haven't been able to get out yet." She handed me a box, which I opened to peek inside. I could see white flannel with tiny red flowers. It was also wrapped in wax paper, which made me laugh.

Henrietta gently slapped my hand down. "No, no, Jo. You must put it under the tree until Christmas," she said jovially.

"I'm not making any promises," I said, and I hugged her hard. "Thank you, Henrietta."

When I got home, I didn't put the present under the tree. I hid it from Mother as best as I could with my body, ran upstairs to my room, and shut the door. I opened the box, pulled out the flannel, and shook it fully open. Beautiful! Just beautiful. It was a white flannel nightgown with tiny red flowers on it. The yoke was edged with fine soft white lace and closed with three little red buttons. It had long sleeves, and it fell to the floor with the hem edged in the lace. I instantly loved it. I think it was the only piece of clothing I ever really really loved. I wore it as often as was humanly possible. I wasn't fully grown when I first received it, but I never outgrew it. The hem rose higher, and the sleeves got shorter, but it still fit a couple of years later. I expected I would wear it forever.

One day, I realized it had not come through the laundry. I looked all over the house for it. It was not in the bathroom hamper. It was nowhere to be found in my dresser or closet. It was not under my bed. I checked Jessie's room and the boy's room too, just in case. I kept on the lookout for it every day for several days. I just couldn't imagine where it was. I asked every person who lived in the house if they had seen it. All said no.

Now ten days had gone by. Mother was standing at the kitchen sink peeling potatoes for lunch. I pulled open the rag drawer that was next to the sink. I wanted to get cleaning rags to help with my Saturday morning chores. To my horror, my hand reached in and pulled out a piece of my precious flannel nightgown from Henrietta. I cried out in shock. The whole thing was there, but it was torn up into at least a dozen pieces. I was devastated. I gathered up all the pieces and began loudly yelling at Mother who just kept peeling potatoes but looked down at me and burst out laughing.

"My nightgown from Henrietta! I have been looking all over for it for days. You knew how much I loved it. How do you have the gall to just take it without my permission and rip it up," I scolded.

"Shut your mouth, or I'll knock you into the middle of next week," snapped Mother. She gave me a kick with her foot.

"You said you hadn't seen it. You lied to me. You had no right to tear it up. It was mine!" I yelled.

"What are you crying about?" she laughingly snarled at me. "That ugly homemade thing was completely outgrown, worn-out, and nothing but a rag left anyway. It belongs in the rag drawer. I put a store-bought one Jessie has outgrown on your pile."

"I don't want a store-bought one! I want this one!" I screamed at her.

The demon in her began to snarl. "Keep your voice down," she hissed.

Clinging to the pieces of flannel, I cringed, but I felt empowered and I screamed at her some more. "You are a liar! I hate you!"

It seemed as if I was watching her in slow motion as she turned to face me with great deliberation and a paring knife in her hand. She had crazy eyes—red blazing eyes. She lifted her right hand as if she was going to stab me. Instinctively, I dropped the flannel and grabbed her wrist. She dropped the potato on the floor, and I grabbed her other wrist. With all my might, I pushed her back to the sink. I was shocked at my own strength.

"James!" she pathetically screamed out.

"Go ahead and scream!" I yelled back at her. "No one else is home."

Adrenalin was pumping through my veins. I was slowly pushing her hand that held the knife toward her own neck. For the first time in my life, I felt like I had the upper hand over her. It was enough. I realized I didn't really want it. In a saving thought, I backed off.

She kept up her laughing growl while I scooped up my torn flannel and ran upstairs to my bedroom.

This hurt worse than physical pain. I can only describe it as heartbreak, and I felt it every night when I put on a different nightgown. The pain went on for days, then weeks, and even months. Yes, it was worn and had a few holes, but it was my favorite and I wore it constantly. This was unthinkable. There were a few things I loved, and this one was precious to me because I felt loved in it. How could she be so cold and unfeeling? She was heartless. I cried all day and cursed her under my breath. It was irreplaceable to me.

Mother must have been jealous that I loved Henrietta even though Henrietta was her best friend. Henrietta was always kind to every person in our family. She knew Mother from school. Mother didn't seem to like Henrietta much, but I couldn't think of any other woman she liked better.

She once told a story about how poor Henrietta had to marry one of her cast-off suitors. I figured he got the best deal then. Because she lived just across the street, I spent time there learning to sew. It was a peaceful haven away from Mother. Henrietta made it so much fun. She made beautiful things, and she never criticized anything I made.

Chapter 10
God, Help Me

I hate sleeping in pants. I thanked God now for this prison-issue nightgown. God. Yes, I believe in God. I had learned the Apostles' Creed from constant repetition in church, and tonight, the words flowed automatically.

"I believe in God, the Father Almighty, the creator of heaven and earth, and in Jesus Christ, his only Son, our Lord, who was conceived of the Holy Spirit, born of the Virgin Mary, suffered under Pontius Pilate, was crucified, died, and was buried. He descended into hell. The third day, he arose again from the dead. He ascended into heaven and sitteth at the right hand of God the Father Almighty, from whence he shall come to judge the living and the dead. I believe in the Holy Spirit, the holy Catholic church, the communion of saints, the forgiveness of sins, the resurrection of the body, and life everlasting. Amen."

"God, help me," I prayed. "Help me remember. Maybe I did do it." I lay still in the dark, trying to think. The color red came to my mind. When I closed my eyes, I could see red all over my hands. I turned them over and back again, watching the red liquid drip from my hands. Maybe I am crazy. I hate the color red. My mother loves red.

Mother told me a story once. I didn't like it.

*****

"The Minnesota State School for Dependent and Neglected Children was built in 1886 right here in Owatonna," she said.

I thought she must be too stupid to know that stories started with, "Once upon a time…"

"For the next fifty-nine years, the school took in orphans," she continued. "Poor little dirty children with no parents from all around the state. Every day, educators at the school taught them the value of exercise, discipline, good behavior, and hard work. Many of the children died at the institution. All the children who died there are buried in the graveyard behind the school. In 1945, one sad day, the orphanage was shut down. Too bad for me or I could take you there."

*****

"Dad," I softly whimpered. "Tell me a better story. I need a drink from the water that saved a princess."

"Come here, Shiny." I heard his laughing voice. It was so real in my mind. He always seemed so happy. In my thoughts, I climbed up on his lap to listen.

Chapter 11
The Redskin

"Have you ever heard about the healing waters in Owatonna?" he began.

"Owatonna," I repeated. "No, I never heard about it," I said.

"Well, as I understand it, Owatonna got its name from a princess."

"A real princess?" I inquired.

"Once upon, a time there was a redskin princess," said Dad. "Princess Owatonna. She was the daughter of a Sioux Indian named Chief Wabena. Little Owatonna loved being a princess. All the Indians in the tribe loved her. She was so beautiful and kind. Her black hair was very shiny because it was pasted with bear oil and braided into the longest braids you ever saw."

"Did they wrap around her head?" I asked, thinking of Henrietta Bjornevik.

"No, Jo, they hung down her back and touched the ground," explained Dad. "One day, Princess Owatonna got sick. The witch doctor for the tribe could find nothing to cure her. He tried lots of things."

"Like what?" I wanted to know.

"Like boiled spider juice," said Dad.

"Icky," I said.

"And baked crushed eagle feathers," continued Dad.

"Yuck." I could only imagine the poor sick princess trying to eat that.

"And rotten loon eggs," added Dad.

"Pew, they would be stinky," I said. *No wonder she couldn't get well*, I thought. "Is Dr. Androvich a witch doctor?" I asked, thinking about his slicked down jet-black hair.

Dad scowled and then just laughed, but he didn't say no.

"So, yes, the princess was very sick and frail," said Dad. "Pretty soon, she couldn't even walk anymore. She told her dad, Chief Wabena, that she was going to die. He was very sad because he loved his little princess so much.

"Then one day, Chief Wabena heard of the healing waters called Minnewaucan, where the waters bubbled up out of the ground. It was by Maple Creek, right next to the Straight River. There is nothing straight about the Straight River, you know. It winds around like this and then like this." His hand snaked around and around to show me what the winding river was like.

"Chief Wabena moved his whole tribe to live right by the waters. Every day, he had the Princess Owatonna drink the healing waters, and sure enough, every day, she got a little better until they healed her completely.

"Many years later, when the white people came to this area, they named the big town after the little princess, Owatonna. She is still there at the waters, you know."

"No, I didn't know that," I said because he paused and waited for my answer.

"Her sweet spirit hovers over the bubbling waters," he continued. "She calls out to weary travelers to stop there and drink of the magical waters. They built a statue of her there."

"Really?" I asked. "Can we go and see it?"

"Yes, we can," he promised. "Some time, I will take you there to see it and have a drink of the waters that saved a princess."

*****

"Drink the water that saves," I whispered it several times. "The water that saves."

Thinking about it tonight, I thought Dad must have meant Jesus because he is the healing water that saves. In the book of

Revelation, the disciple John was shown by the risen Christ "a pure river of water of life, clear as crystal, proceeding out of the throne of God and of the Lamb."[4]

With that comforting thought, I fell asleep.

---

[4] Revelation 22:1 (NKJV)

Chapter 12
Testing the Boundaries

Tuesday, September 3, Early Morning

Blaaaaat! Blaaaaat! Blat blat! Two long blasts and two short ones from the piercing horn awakened me abruptly. I opened my eyes, but I did not move. It took me a minute to realize where I was. I could see it was still dark outside. With dread, I remembered the events of the previous day. I was in jail—that I knew. I had been visited by a psychiatrist who suggested I murdered my mother. The reality was that throughout my short life so far, there were many times I had wished she were dead, and there were a few times I actually did think about killing her.

Did she also say my dad was missing? Well, I have been in jail for at least twenty-four hours, and I have had no word from him. Maybe that is somehow true too. My thoughts were so confused.

Why am I in jail? Why can't I remember any recent events? Why would I need a psychiatrist? I pondered the questions.

"Step away from the door!" blared the loudspeaker. "Step out, and step into the line!"

That awful blaring loudspeaker was getting on my nerves. I supposed it was the breakfast call. I was not hungry, so I did not move. I hated breakfast food anyway. The smell of pancakes or bacon and eggs sticking to my hair for the rest of the day was a nauseating thought.

Why can't they just bring me coffee? I wondered. "I'm skipping breakfast today," I decided.

"Step out, and step into the line!" blared the speaker again.

I rolled over and ignored it.

"#05135775! Step out, and step into the line!" I heard it, but I still did not move. I chose to wait and see what would happen. It wasn't long. A few moments later, a prison matron stepped into my cell and pulled my blanket off. I sat up.

"Get up, and get dressed," she said matter-of-factly.

"Why?" I asked, feeling I had a right to ask questions.

Whack! Right across my cheek with the baton. That stung. It happened so fast I had no time to react. That was the answer to my question. My cheek was now hot with a stinging blow. I leaped up and got dressed as fast as I could. I stepped into the line that was still waiting for me. I heard muffled snickering all across the line.

"That was entertaining," whispered #11284774, chuckling at me.

"Yeah, let's give her the Emmy for the day," whispered #24656776.

I put my head down as I walked, knowing my face was as red as a tomato.

Thoughts of Mother flooded my memory, thinking about another time that my face hurt. I can bring up the long ago past quick as a wink. Why can't I remember two days ago?

CHAPTER 13
THE RED FACE

The summer of 1956 was winding down, and I was preparing myself for a big event—elementary school. My babyhood had come to an end a long time ago. I had turned six in May, and I would be going straight to the first grade because there was no kindergarten in this town yet. I couldn't wait.

"Thankfully," my mother had said, "due to the low population of Germans in the state, the Department of Education has not been able to institute kindergarten here in Havana." She insisted that she, with stick in hand, was the best tutor possible for her preschool children.

"Kindergarten is the German's invention to get rid of their children early. It is just a government babysitter. Those poverty-stricken immigrants always need help from the government. I don't take charity," she said haughtily.

I did not understand her comment about the low population of Germans because she was always complaining about there being far too many Germans around.

Up to now, Mother had been my main teacher, and most of the lessons I had learned from her were joy stealers. The idea of getting away from her and going to school was beyond exciting. If only I could have gone to kindergarten last year, like the rest of the five-year-olds in other states, I would have been spared a year of her abuse. At the time, I did not know it was abuse. I just thought all mothers slapped, spanked, and humiliated their children constantly.

Henrietta is nice, I thought. In my heart, I knew Mrs. Bjornevik would always be nice to everyone. I guessed it was because she didn't have any children.

Little Jimmy with the jet-black hair would have to stay home with Mother all by himself now. That's what Dad called him—"Little Jimmy with the jet-black hair."

Poor boy. I knew it was pretty easy for me to make her angry by the things I did, but she got angry just looking at Jimmy. He had burn scars all over his face, hands, and arms. His thin jet-black hair was patchy on the top of his scarred head too.

When he first came into the world, I was just barely three years old. The family talked about a new baby coming. I did not know where it was coming from. I did know Mother was getting a huge tummy, but no one was allowed to mention it. I had heard a neighbor lady say the word *pregnant* at one of Mother's tea/coffee parties. I tried the word out for myself one day because I was standing eye level with Mother's huge protuberance.

"Are you pregnant?" I asked, having absolutely no clue what the word might mean. Her hand was on autopilot when I was around. I didn't see it coming.

Whack. It backhanded my forehead, and I fell backward, causing the chair behind me to dig into my back. Double whammy.

"Don't you ever let me hear you say that word in public again," she said. She sounded just disgusted with it. I felt my face flush red. I got up as fast as I could and ran to my room so she wouldn't see me cry. I didn't want to get "something else to cry about."

Pregnant? I mulled the word over and over in my mind. *It must be in the dirty word list*, I decided, storing it away with the other bad words I had collected in my few years of life but was determined to find the meaning of it one day.

Two weeks before the baby arrived, Mother and Dad were discussing a name for it at the supper table.

"How about Jennifer, if it's a girl?" Mother had offered, but James knew it was firm.

I looked at Jessica and Johnny. Johnny wasn't as mean as Jessica. "I hope it is a boy," I said as I stared at Jessica with a wrinkled up nose.

"How about James, after me, if it is a boy?" asked Dad.

"I like James," I offered, smiling up at my dad. He patted me on the head. I like my dad.

"Pshaw. Not another James," said Sandra. I thought maybe she didn't like my dad. I thought maybe she doesn't like anybody. "I like Jackson," she said.

"Jack, hmmm," said Dad, sounding defeated and looking wounded. I have always paid very close attention to the look on a face. I can read the eyes. He didn't like it, but he gave in. He always gave in to her. I hated giving in to her.

The day the baby was born, Dad bragged about him to Jessie, Johnny, and me right away, proudly declaring, "We named him Jackson James Lewis." Then he asked us, "What do you think of a new baby brother? You can call him Jack."

"No!" I screamed out and stomped my foot. "His name is Jimmy! My baby brother's name is Jimmy." I declared it. I was adamant about it. I insisted on it. No matter what anyone else said or suggested, I screamed out, "His name is Jimmy!" I had obstinately and constantly demanded it until every argument about it ceased. I think now, somehow, I was defending my dad.

His name is Jimmy. I thought I won that one, but years, later I would realize it was Dad who won it, not me. They named him James Jackson Lewis.

Yet poor Jimmy, undeniably.

"Ein dah one dat gotted buuned," he said to every single person who came to the door. At just eighteen months of age, he did indeed get badly burned. It was not my fault.

I did not like taking a bath. I was afraid of water. I was terrified when Mother washed my hair and poured water over my head. I was sure I was going to drown. I especially hated it when Mother put Jimmy into the tub with me. I thought his boy body parts were disgusting.

It was Saturday night, bath night, December 11, at six thirty in the evening. We still lived with Grandmother Lewis. Mother, without thinking about what she was doing, turned on the hot water faucet in the tub, preparing to put me in it with Jimmy. He was standing next to the tub, naked and excited to get into it. I was sitting on the closed toilet seat, fully clothed, waiting until the last minute to strip and hop in.

The hot water was always turned on first and allowed to run for quite a long while before adding the cold because it took time to heat up. That's the way it always was until a couple of days ago. Dad had the idea to fix it because Mother complained the water was never hot enough. James discovered the hot water tank temperature was set at a very low heat, probably because Grandmother Lewis was cheap. Unaware of any consequences, he turned it up as high as it would go. Now it was scalding hot. He was proud that he fixed it and was happy to tell Sandra. Maybe she could stop complaining about it now.

"Be careful with it now," said James to Sandra. "You could get burned."

"I like it hot," she said, flirting with him.

"That's my doll," he said, flirting back. "But I'm talking about the hot water."

This night, the water came out hot right away. It was steaming, something new to Jimmy, and it fascinated him. Dad came out of his office to ask Mother a question. I do not remember what it was; no one does.

I don't know if I said it before, but Mother was very beautiful to men. Personally, I did not like her looks. If looks can be cruel, that is what she looked like to me. Dad, however, liked her looks. He said I looked just like her, only lighter hair. I couldn't see it.

He looked her up and down, completely forgetting what it was he wanted because now he was feeling like he wanted something else. He pulled her into the hallway where he pressed her up against the wall and began kissing her. It was nothing new. I had seen it many times before. It disgusted me. He reached up and grabbed a breast.

"James!" she squealed.

"Yuck," I said as I swung the bathroom door shut so I would not have to see it.

Mother broke away from the embrace and opened the door just as Jimmy was diving head first into the tub and directly under the raging hot water faucet.

"Jimmy!" she screamed at the top of her lungs.
"Waaaah!" Jimmy screamed at the top of his lungs.
"Dad!" I screamed at the top of my lungs.
"Oh my God!" Dad screamed at the top of his lungs.

Jimmy was rushed to the hospital with severe burns from the top of his head to his waist. Dr. Androvich immediately took control of his care and spent every free minute he had in Jimmy's room. It was three weeks before Jimmy could come home. Fortunately, he still took a baby bottle that kept him from getting dehydration. When I think about it, I think he still took a baby bottle until he was five years old.

Mother slept there with him, and Grandmother Lewis helped Dad at home. The day they brought Jimmy home, he still had his little hands and arms wrapped up in bandages. His head was scabbed up, and his baby face was very red with peeling skin, as if sunburned very badly. Everyone felt so sorry for him and catered to his every whim.

Dad said it was Mother's fault for not watching the baby. Mother said it was Dad's fault for distracting her.

Mother said it was Dad's fault for turning the water temperature up too high. Dad said it was Mother's fault for not adding the cold the water right away.

Dad said it was Mother's fault because she dressed too sexy. Mother said it was Dad's fault because all he ever wanted was sex.

Mother said it was Dad's fault because he wanted to punish her. Dad said if he did want to punish her, he could think of a better way to do it than that.

They didn't talk normally to each other anymore. They screamed blame back and forth for days after until Mother said, "It's Jo's fault for shutting the bathroom door."

Dad never said another word about it. That really hurt my feelings. Usually, I would like to hurt Jimmy, but that day, I did not.

It was not my fault.

CHAPTER 14
THE RED MILK CARTON

After I sat down with the other prisoners at the breakfast table. I put my hand on my cheek. It was burning hot. I didn't dare look up at anyone of the other inmates. I knew they were all still snickering about me.

Well, I learned two lessons, I guess. Don't ask questions, and follow the rules.

I looked at my tray for the first time. Egg and something scramble, dry toast, and a small carton of milk. It looked okay, so I took a bite. That was a mistake.

I spit the bite out into my napkin. I would not be able to take another bite of that. I ate the toast and stared at the carton of milk. I have always hated milk. I picked up the red waxed carton to see if it was cold. Just as I suspected. It was not cold enough. I sat back a little, wanting distance from the scrambled yuck.

"Are you going to eat that?" said #24656776 quietly.

"No. It is disgusting," I said.

"Good," she said as she quickly swapped trays with me. She ate every bite.

She must be like a dog, I thought. Dogs can eat anything.

I turned the milk carton around in my hand, trying to decide if I could drink it, and memories took control again.

*****

I had finally joined the ranks of school children across the land, along with Jessie and Johnny. I felt pretty much grown-up already. I admit I did not play well with other children my age. For some reason, I felt much more mature. I couldn't tolerate babyishness. I wonder where I got that from?

On the first day of first grade, for some strange reason, Mother declared she would see me there. I insisted I had played there in the playground all summer, and I knew how to get there without getting lost. She easily relented but then insisted Jessie and Johnny should take me there, hand in hand, and show me to my room.

I already knew where my room was. Dad had taken me to "round up" in the summer, and we met the teacher, Mrs. Lovdahl. She was big with fat legs and tons of red hair. I was so surprised when I first saw her. She was the first person I knew with red hair. I didn't know for sure hair could be red. I had heard my mother complain about people with red hair as if they had a disease.

With her nose wrinkled up with aversion, she would say, "Redheads are always so pale and freckly." Or, "I never did like a ginger child." Or, "I believe redheads must have some sort of chromosome damage."

I decided to keep my opinion neutral until I saw a negative of my own.

I wonder if she has children, I thought after meeting her. So far, from her demeanor, I could not tell. I kept a close watch on her, looking for any flaws.

James was the only dad there that day. All the other kids had their mommies with them. They seemed quite excited, but I was totally bored. I figured they were all babies and needed their mommies. I sure didn't need or want my mother, and I was no baby. I could not understand the concept of this silly event or its purpose.

Many of the mothers were talking to Dad, laughing and smiling at him. They seemed much more interested in him than they did in Mrs. Lovdhal.

Mrs. Lovdhal struggled to keep attention focused on herself. Dad was a very handsome man. He was only five foot ten inches tall, but he had a lot of muscles, huge brown eyes, brown wavy hair, and a smile that melted you. He laughed at everything the women said to him.

On the first day of school, I was surprised as Jessie and Johnny agreed with Mother. Each took a hand of mine and marched me out the door. Since when were they willing to help me? Halfway down the first block, they felt they were safe from Mother's spying eyes, and they dropped my hands like hot cakes and began making fun of me. They had learned a lesson and were teaching it to me. Always agree with Mother and then out of her sight, do whatever you want.

"Jo is a baby. Nah nah nah nah nah nah," sang Jessie over her shoulder as she ran ahead of me.

"I...I...I hope you get lost," stuttered Johnny as he sped after her.

I was used to being spurned by them, but it still hurt anyway.

I decided I was proud to walk by myself. I spotted my best friend, Martine Kleven, walking on the other side of the street. I don't know why I called her my best friend. I often avoided playing with her and dissed her more often than not. She was holding her mother's hand. At first, I thought Martine was a big baby. Then I felt curiously jealous.

To my surprise, I hated the first grade right from the start. The joy of being away from Mother was not enough to make a school day enjoyable. Every day, I told Dad I hated school.

Every day, he would say, "I don't understand how a little girl could not like school where she will learn to read and write."

Most of this hate came because I did not like the teacher, Mrs. Lovdahl.

"I'm sure she has children," I told my mother.

"What does that have to do with it?" Mother asked, wrinkling up her brow like I had just told her a completely far-fetched idiom. I did not answer because I knew she would not understand my explanation.

Mrs. Lovdahl was a very large person, which was very intimidating to me, but then maybe it wasn't her size that I didn't like. After all, Henrietta was a very large person, and I liked her a lot. Maybe it was because she was the first person I knew, since my mother, to make me do things I did not want to do. I disliked being inside the schoolhouse most of the day. I often found myself looking out the windows, wishing I were out there in the sunshine and enjoying nature.

No thanks to the USDA, my school had instituted the "milk for all school children" nutrition program, trying to contribute to the health and nourishment of the underprivileged. I knew I was not underprivileged. Mother would often tell me how spoiled I was.

Mother said the milk program was charity from the government, and we did not take charity. That is why I did not understand why she insisted I take in my penny every day to pay for the milk. All the other kids paid for theirs too. It came packaged in a red waxed carton, and by the time it ended up on my desk, it was room temperature, never cold enough.

"Drink your milk, Jo," Mrs. Lovdahl would say at milk break. I hated milk. To me, it tasted sour every single day. At the first sip, I would gag and try not to throw up.

"It is sour," I complained to the teacher.

She would smell my carton and say, "It is not sour."

"I hate milk," I would respond.

"Everyone likes milk," she would say to me as if I was lying because I didn't.

Finally, when everyone was done drinking theirs, I would throw out as much of mine as I could get away with. By the time I reached second grade, I had learned to keep the penny and refuse the milk entirely. It was such a brilliant idea that I was disappointed with myself that I had not thought of it a year earlier. If I saved five pennies, I could buy a candy bar.

After lunch, Mrs. Lovdahl said, "Put your head on your desk now, and take a little nap."

The desk was hard. "Nap time? Oh brother," I complained, wrinkling up my brow with surprised disgust. How was a little girl supposed to take a nap on that? I wanted to know. I was not tired either. I did not want to rest in school. I was a big girl, and naps were for babies. Why didn't she know I came to school to get away from naps. Well, mostly Mother, but naps too.

The teacher is so stupid, I thought. *I can't learn anything sitting here, looking at the wall.*

I watched all the other children obediently lay their heads down on their desks. My head was the last one down. After catching Mrs. Lovdahl glaring at me, I decided I would lay it down, but I certainly wasn't going to close my eyes. I looked at all the submissive children pretending to be asleep and decided I might have to find a good reason to quit school.

That's when I saw him. He was a year ahead of me. This would be the only year we shared a classroom. Robert Hoffman was three desks over, sitting in the second-grade section. His head was down, but his green eyes were wide open. He was looking right at me. The instant my eyes locked on his, he broke out into a big smile. He brought his hand up to the desktop and gave me a little wave. Oh, I didn't know boys could be cute. Maybe naptime wasn't so bad. I guess I will stay in school after all.

CHAPTER 15

THE RED NECKTIE

Tuesday, September 3, After Breakfast

My mind came back to prison and the long table filled with women prisoners. I opened the carton of milk and drank it as fast as I could. Not because I liked it but because I was hungry. This time, I did not gag, and I felt some victory in that.

"Robert," I spoke his name out loud, feeling a deep longing to be with him, and that got me a quick elbow to the side from #11284774.

"Why are you so mean?" I whispered.

"What are you talking about?" #11284774 whispered back. "You are the only murderer in this whole prison."

On the march back to my cell, I meditated on the names I loved to call him. Robber Bobber, Robbob, Robo, Berty, Hurdy Gurdy Man. The US Army, with its enlistment advertisements, had taken my Robber Bobber away from me for a while. He was brave. I loved him for that. He wanted to help his country. I loved him for that too. I prayed every day he would not be sent to Vietnam. That thought was terrifying. How could I ever be happy if anything happened to him?

Now back in my cell, the door slams shut. So much metal clanging against metal around here hurts my psyche. I shouldn't be here. Yeah. Prison. Seems like I just got out of Mother's prison, and now find myself in this one. People controlling other people makes me so mad.

I heard steps coming down the hall. They sounded different from Dr. Westfield, and they stopped at my door.

"Jo Lewis?" a man called through the door.

"Yes," I said as I got up and backed away to sit on my cot.

The door opened, and a man stepped in dressed in a nice black suit with a white shirt and red necktie. I stared at the necktie, not wanting to look at his face. It made me feel uneasy. He seemed familiar. Flashes of previous conversation zipped through my mind.

"What happened?" he had yelled at me.

"I don't know!" I had yelled back.

"What did you do?" he asked.

"What did I do?" I asked.

He had a small stool in his hand so we could both sit at the table.

"May we sit and talk for a while?" he asked.

I nodded my permission and desperately tried to think of how I knew him.

"Do you remember me?" he asked.

"No, but you seem familiar," I said.

I spoke with Dr. Westfield yesterday, and she indicated you might have some loss of memory," he said.

"Should I know you?" I questioned.

"My name is Jacob Sanders, remember? We spoke three days ago when you were first brought in here," he said.

"Hmmm. Sorry, I don't remember you, but something does seem familiar. The red necktie seems familiar," I answered.

"I am your defense attorney," he explained.

"Do I need a defender?" I meekly asked.

"Yes. You were arrested." He was matter-of-fact.

"I don't remember, but I guess it is pretty obvious because here I am in jail." I felt so weary. "Have I been here three days really? I don't know why I can't remember." I blinked several times, as if clearing my eyes would clear my brain.

"Well, you have been through a pretty traumatic experience. After I saw you on Saturday, I asked Dr. Westfield to come and evaluate your mental health. She believes you have psychogenic amnesia," he said.

"And just what is that?" I asked.

"I will read to you what she says in her report. I am just learning about it myself." Then he continued. "'Psychogenic amnesia is a disorder characterized by abnormal memory functioning. It results from the effects of severe stress or psychological trauma on the brain, rather than from any physical or physiological cause. It is equivalent to the clinical condition known as repressed memory syndrome.'

"'I believe Jo Lewis has situation-specific amnesia, a type of psychogenic amnesia that occurs as a result of a severely stressful event. It is most commonly associated with a violent experience involving emotional shock, such as being mugged or raped or involved in car crash. Those at increased risk include those sexually or physically abused during childhood or those who have experienced domestic violence, natural disasters, terrorist acts. Essentially, anyone who has experienced any sufficiently severe psychological stress, internal conflict, or intolerable life situation.'

"'Freudian psychology suggests psychogenic amnesia is an act of self-preservation, where the alternative might be overwhelming anxiety or even suicide. Unpleasant, unwanted, or psychologically dangerous memories are repressed or blocked from entering the consciousness as a kind of subconscious self-censorship, but they remain in the unconscious. Repressed memories may be accessed by psychotherapy, hypnotism, or other techniques, although it is often difficult to distinguish a true repressed memory from a false one without corroborating evidence.'"[5]

"Do you understand all that?" I questioned him.

"Well, I am going to try because if you can't really remember, it will be a line of defense," he said.

"Believe me, I wish I could remember. I want to go home." I sighed deeply. "Jacob is a nice name."

"Thanks," Jacob responded.

"All the names in my family begin with *J*," I added.

---

[5] ©2010 by Luke Mastin (www.human-memory.net)

"That's nice. I have questions I need to ask you. Can we just go right at it? Maybe something will jog your memory." He didn't seem to want any small talk.

"Okay," I relented.

"The police found you at Salet's Department Store on Saturday, late in the afternoon," he began. "Do you remember that?"

"I have a job at Salet's." I corroborated. "I love working there. It is the only store in Owatonna that has the newest fashions. What day is it today?" I really had no idea.

"Today is Tuesday, September 3, so three days ago was Saturday, August 31," he responded.

"That could be right. I bring dad coffee every Saturday at six thirty. It's nothing special, just a cup of gas station coffee. We walk his dog, Blackie, before I go to work," I said.

*****

Thinking of Blackie made me smile. All of Dad's dogs were named Blackie. Whenever one black dog died, he would get another black one. The first one I can remember was his second dog. I remember laying in the grass in the side yard of the big house. It was a cool day, but I didn't feel it because the sun was shining. I was using Blackie as a pillow. I petted him as long as he would lay there. When he finally got up and wandered off, I looked at my hands. I was surprised they were so dirty.

In my baby mentality, I said, "So that's why Dad calls him Blackie."

I don't think he ever got a bath. No need, I guess, as Mother never allowed any of the dogs in the house.

"Wash your hands after you touch that filthy animal!" I could hear her screeching at me. She said dogs belonged on farms where they were useful and should never be allowed in town.

One time, Dad took his dinner plate with leftovers on it outside and set it on the porch for Blackie to have a treat. When Mother realized what he had done, she threw out the nice glass dinner plate instead of washing it, insisting it was ruined.

*****

"Do you remember doing that three days ago?"

"Washing my hands?" I dumbly asked, being brought back from my thoughts.

"No, walking the dog," he seemed so surprised at my offbeat comment.

"Three days ago..." I struggled to think. "It seems like the last time I went there, the dog greeted me at the door. I was alarmed to see him inside the house. He had bloody footprints."

Flashes of Blackie all excited and making bloody footprints hurt my brain.

"I felt horrible for him. I love Blackie. I thought he hurt his feet or something. Why would he leave bloody footprints?" I asked.

"What did you do?" Jacob asked.

"I don't remember." I said.

"What happened to your face? I didn't see that the other day." He reached out to almost touch my blazing hot cheek, but I backed away.

"I got my a lesson in following orders." I put my hand over it.

He pulled a small flash camera out of his suit pocket. It was a Kodak Instamatic, just like the one Robert gave me for Christmas. He pulled my hand down, then quickly snapped a picture of my cheek.

"I am going to report this," he said.

"Oh no. Please don't. Just let it go. I don't want to get in more trouble. I learned long ago in life to keep my ailments to myself."

I just drifted off again, thinking of how I learned that lesson.

Chapter 16
The Red Snow Suit

In the first three weeks of school, I had mastered the Dick and Jane Pre-Primers, "We Look and See," "We Come and Go," and "We work and Play." Mrs. Lovdahl then put me in the advanced circle with the few elite of the class. I loved reading. I had finished "Fun with Dick and Jane" by the time the first snow fell.

I well remember the first snowfall that year. It was Thursday morning, November 15. As soon as I opened my eyes, I knew something felt different in the air. I could actually smell it. I ran to the window to look out, and I was dazzled. I saw the most beautiful sight I thought I had ever seen. Five inches of gorgeous light and fluffy snow had softly fallen during the night. Now the clouds were gone, and the grass, the trees, the houses, and pretty much everything I could see was covered with snow. It was sparkling everywhere. With excitement, I ran downstairs in my nightgown to tell anyone who might be up. In the kitchen, I found Jessie listening to the radio.

"It snowed last night, Jessie. Come and look out the window," I invited her to share in my pleasure.

"I already saw it, stupid," Jessie answered.

"What are you doing?" I asked because she was sitting on the counter, an activity that was strictly forbidden.

"I'm waiting to hear if our school might be closed for a snow day," she said.

"What's a snow day?" I asked. I had not learned about that yet.

"Shh," she shushed me.

We listened intently together. There were some closings. Our school, Havana, would be close to the beginning of the list. We were not on the list. It would take a lot more snow than a fluffy five inches to shut down these hardy Minnesotans. Jessie snapped off the radio.

"Yay!" I cheered.

"What are you cheering about, idiot?" questioned Jessie.

"I don't want to stay home," I said.

"I thought you hated school," said Jessie.

"I do, but staying home with Mother is worse." Sometimes I was too quick to speak the truth.

"You're a moron. I'm going to tell Mother what you said," threatened Jessie.

"I'll tell her you said stupid," I threatened right back.

"She won't believe you because you are stupid," said Jessie as she ran out of the room and up stairs to wake up Johnny.

I followed her up and got dressed for school. I ate my breakfast cereal, all the while wishing breakfast would be outlawed. I put on my coat and opened the front door to go out.

"Come back here, Jo," said Mother, with the voice that dug into the back of your neck. It made my shoulders tighten up to the back of my head.

"It is cold outside, and snow is on the ground. You will have to wear snow pants to keep your legs warm when you walk to school," she continued.

Snowfall was usually exciting, but this day, it was an unfortunate event because it brought an unfortunate outfit out of the winter coat closet. Mother was very particular about her own clothes. She was very particular about mine as well. It didn't matter if I hated something that she wanted me to wear. If she loved it, that was all that mattered, no matter how awful it was to me.

"Snow pants? Yuck, they are so ugly," I whined. "And red? I hate red."

"Put them on. They are warm." Mother said it with that look in her eyes that made me nervous.

Obediently, I sat down on the floor and put one foot into the pant leg. "They're itchy and scratchy. They are wool. I am allergic to wool. I don't want to wear them," I continued to whine.

"They are very stylish," said Mother. "They are lamb's wool and very soft."

"They are not soft. They are scratchy," I complained.

They came with matching coat and bonnet. Right away, I could see they would be just as hard to get off once I got to school as they were to get on.

"Stylish, my foot," I muttered. The Shirley Temple ensemble was downright hideous. I was only six years old, but I knew what looked good. I knew they were for a baby, and I knew that she knew that I was no baby. She told me often enough.

"What did you say?" snapped Mother. She was losing her patience fast.

"I said my other foot is stuck. Are you deaf?" I snapped back.

That comment exceeded her limit of tolerance. A crisp, stinging slap came my way, landing square on my cheek and throwing my head to the side. Instinctively, my hands reached up and covered my face. The stricken cheek was blazing hot.

"Don't you ever speak to me that way again!" she snarled. I was thinking she was snarling like a mad dog.

Grandmother Lewis read Fred Gipson's book, *Old Yeller*, to Jessie and Johnny this past summer. I had listened in to the entire book even if I was not invited to sit next to her while she read some of it every day after lunch. Old Yeller got rabies from trying to protect his beloved family from a rabid wolf, and he was growling and snarling and foaming at the mouth. He had become a mad dog, and now everybody was afraid of him. Snarl or not, I was determined to not be afraid of her.

The inconvenient over-the-shoulder straps of the itchy snow pants somehow buckled in the front to hold them up. Mother finally helped me after I struggled for ten minutes. I refused to look at her. Now I was suited and booted up and shoved out the door.

"Why did you shove me?" I complained. "You hurt my neck."

"Because you are going to be late for school if you keep this up," she complained right back. "Now get out there, and get the stink blown off you."

When I got outside, I put the sleeve of my coat to my nose and smelled it. She was right about that. It stunk.

The five block walk to school seemed a lot farther now, trudging through the snow. I was sure it was the fault of the snow pants. My feet were heavy. My whole body itched. My head was sweating, and my mitten-covered fingers couldn't scratch a thing.

In the school building and just outside the classroom was a coatroom. Each child entered there to remove all their outer garments and hang them up on hooks before going inside to the classroom. All of the other children seemed to easily disrobe and hang up their stuff. Not me though. I was so embarrassed. I knew all the kids were looking at me. The first warning bell rang. Usually, I was in my seat by the first bell.

What kind of ugly outfit is that? I knew they were all thinking. I felt my cheeks. They were burning hot, so I knew they were red, especially the one that had been slapped. I did not say hi to any of my friends, and none of them said hi to me, not even Martine. Maybe they didn't recognize me. It took me ten minutes to get the bonnet and coat off. The double-breasted buttons were way too big for the buttonholes. Then I began struggling with the red snow pants. I could absolutely not get them unfastened. While I kept trying, the second bell rang. That meant everyone was to find their seat immediately or Mrs. Lovdahl would scold them. Everyone did find their own seat except for me. Those red snow pants were so embarrassing. They were ruining my life.

How could Mother think they were attractive? I'm sure she didn't really. She was just punishing me. She was probably home right this minute, sitting at the kitchen table, sipping her tea and laughing at my predicament, remembering I had shut the bathroom door on her and Dad when Jimmy got burned. I was getting what I deserved.

"That'll teach her a lesson." I pictured her in my mind, throwing her head back and laughing like an evil villain. "Ha-ha-ha!"

"I don't know why she hates me, but I hate her just as much," I muttered under my breath. Soon I heard the teacher calling the roll call.

"Barbara?" said Mrs. Lovdahl.

"Here," said Barbara.

"Dougie?" said Mrs. Lovdahl.

"Here," said Dougie.

"Martine?" said Mrs. Lovdahl.

"Here," said Martine.

"Jo?" said Mrs. Lovdahl. Everyone was quiet and looked around the room for me.

"Where's Jo?" asked Mrs. Lovdahl.

Martine obnoxiously volunteered. "She is here somewhere. I'm sure I saw her in the coatroom."

Uh-oh. There was that icky feeling now in the pit of my stomach. I simply could not handle the embarrassment of not being able to get those ugly, itchy red snow pants off, and now, because of that blabbermouth Martine, the teacher knew I was somewhere in the vicinity, struggling like a baby.

I began to cry, softly at first. That didn't work. Big, fat Mrs. Lovdahl didn't hear me. Since I felt like a baby, I might as well be a baby, so I began to wail loudly. This brought her running to me, where I was sitting on the floor in the corner of the coatroom.

"Jo," she said with feigned compassion. "What is the matter?"

"I'm sick," I lied. "My tummy hurts. I have to throw up."

"Oh dear," said Mrs. Lovdahl. She felt my head. "You do feel hot. What's that mark on you cheek?" I did not answer. "Maybe it is a rash. You will just have to put your coat back on and go back home."

Instantly, I felt a smile creep in behind my eyes.

How about that, I thought. *I get to go home.*

Mrs. Lovdahl helped me get suited and booted up, but she seemed really annoyed with the whole ordeal. I heard the loud tsking and sighing and noted the shaking of the head.

"Mrs. Lovdahl, do you have any children?" I asked.

"Why, yes, I do, Jo. I have a boy and a girl." She changed her frown to a smile and added, "I love children. That is why I decided to be a teacher."

There it was, the answer to my questioning mind, and just as I had suspected. She was mean. She had children. Somehow the two went hand in hand.

I thought the idea of going home was a great idea until I actually left the building and headed for my house. Lumbering through the snow, I began to dread what I might have to face once I got there.

When I reached the front steps, I looked up and saw Mother behind the window of the door, waiting just inside there for me. The school had called to tell her to expect me.

She opened the door and harshly said, "What's the matter with you."

"I'm sick?" I said it as a question, hoping she would fall for it. She glared at me. "My tummy hurts?" I clarified.

"Go get into bed, but leave your clothes on until I call Dr. Androvich and see if he can see you," she said, pointing to the stairwell.

Oh no, not the dreaded Dr. Androvich. My thoughts were ablaze with the embarrassing visits to his office where I was always stripped down and examined. *How did I get myself into this fix?*

Dr. Androvich needs no introduction for Mother. Every time they are together, they act like they are best friends. She calls him Dr. Andro, and he calls her Allessandra. He is very tall with jet-black hair. Dad once called him the world's tallest leprechaun, but Mother royally chewed him out for his lack of discretion and knowledge. She said Dr. Androvich was a Christian Croatian and very well-educated, unlike some other people she knew, referring to my dad, who winced when she said it.

Anyway, Mother was absolutely fanatical about Dr. Androvich. I found it very odd. She said he was a family practitioner with expertise in every aspect of the medical field. I thought he could be better described as an unwelcomed prober of body orifices, but he had brought me successfully into the world even though I was breech, a feat to carry bragging rights, I guess.

To me Dr. Androvich was a tall, gloomy man and very unfriendly, but Mother said he was about as close to God as a man could get. I knew that couldn't be right. I knew angels were close to God and I knew Henrietta was almost an angel and I knew Dr. Androvich was nothing like Henrietta.

I thought he was closer to Adolf Hitler. At that age, I didn't know much about Adolf Hitler, but I did know Gramma Lewis called him "a bad German."

Mother loved it if you had a physical complaint because that meant a trip to see Dr. Androvich or at least a chat on the phone with him. He would always tell her some funny little story, and she would throw her head back and laugh. She always fake-smiled in his presence, and he fake-smiled back. Ugh, I couldn't stand it. She was flirting. But I did not know what flirting was, so I couldn't really describe it at that time.

I could always figure out that Mother was going to see Dr. Androvich or taking someone else to see him when she put on nylons in the middle of the week. Nylons were worn by her for only special occasions like weddings, funerals, or a visit to Dr. Androvich's office. So if it wasn't some kind of party, it was a Dr. Androvich day, and that was a party for her.

I heard the muffled voice of Mother on the phone. Of course, you could never get directly through to the doctor. Mother called the office, left a message, and waited for his return phone call. I was unable to relax, waiting to see what would happen to me. Mother had this certain rapport with him that she could tell him what she wanted, and he would deliver. She could diagnose just about anything, and to my amazement, he believed her, the patient being sight unseen. He would then tell her the appropriate prescription would be waiting at the drugstore for her. Hopefully, that would be my case today.

All too soon, she came upstairs, went to her room where she retrieved a pair of nylons from her dresser drawer, and rolled them up her sexy legs. I didn't know what sexy meant, but that's what Dad said they were. I really thought they were just hairy, and I hoped I would never get black hair on my legs like hers. From my bed, I could see her sitting on the edge of her bed across the hall, snapping the nylons into the garter belt.

Shoot. I knew what that meant—an actual visit to Dr. Androvich. I was really unlucky today. He wanted to see me.

Dad brought the 1952 Greenbrier Green Ford Mainline Tudor Sedan home for us.

"Want me to drive you?" James hollered at the door.

"No need!" Sandra hollered back.

"Lot of snow out there," he said factually.

"No need," repeated Sandra. She knew he did not trust her driving.

"Put Jo in the back then so she is safe," he ordered.

"You're not my father," she threw back at him.

"Go slow. The roads are icy," he advised.

"I know how to drive!" she shouted back at him.

"I don't think you do!" he yelled back at her. Then he turned around and walked the four blocks back to work. She was smiling. He was not.

*****

It was because of me that dad traded in his beloved 1931 Brewster Green Ford Model A Five-Window Coupe for a brand new 1952 Greenbrier Green Ford Mainline Tudor Sedan.

We were all still living at Grandmother Lewis's house. I was two years old. Even though Mother and Grandmother Lewis despised each other, there were some advantages for mother. One was that Grandmother Lewis was a built-in babysitter. Of course, she would only look after Jessie and Johnny. That is why I ended up alone with Mother in the Model A, one day in the summer of 1952. Mother did not like fast driving when James was driving, but when she was alone and thought no one was looking, she sped around just to amuse herself.

That particular day, I was standing on the front seat next to the passenger door. As she sped around one corner, my door flew open. Because I was leaning against it, I flew out of the car and rolled helplessly into the ditch. I was scratched and bruised from head to toe, bleeding and muddy, but fortunately, no broken bones or head injuries. Mother slammed on the brakes, backed the car up, got out, picked me up, threw me back in, told me to stop crying because she was sure I was okay, and took me home. Once in the driveway, she got out of the car, set me on the ground, grabbed the sack of groceries, and went into the house. Still crying, I toddled in after her.

Dad came nonchalantly down from his office in the upstairs of Grandmother's house to greet us, but when he saw me, he began yelling at Sandra. Together, they took me in to see Dr. Androvich where he declared I would live. I was just a toddler, but their fighting words are still with me.

"You tried to kill her," James accused her.

"Don't be ridiculous. It was an accident." Sandra defended herself.

"You were driving too fast." He pointed a finger at her.

"Your car is just old and unsafe." She turned and punched him in the chest.

"How could a baby fall out of a moving car anyway?" he yelled.

"She didn't get hurt. She is fine!" yelled Sandra.

"You never did like her." He was angry.

"Why should I? She is your baby." She was angry.

"It takes two to make a baby." He defended himself.

"Not that time it didn't." She accused him.

They said it all in front of me, thinking I wouldn't remember. But I did. I can remember every single day of the past. Why can't I remember three days ago?

While we were waiting for Dr. Androvich in his office, I touched a large picture that was hanging on the wall and left it hanging slightly crooked. I tried to put it back straight to no avail. He walked in wearing a red necktie tucked into his lab coat. That was the first thing I noticed. Of course, the first thing he noticed was the slightly crooked picture, so before even greeting my mother, he scolded me for touching the frame. How did he know I had touched it? I was the recipient of his heartlessness.

Wow, I thought with instantly embarrassed feelings. *He must have children.* I knew my cheeks were red.

After the things he did to me on the table and the invasion on my body cavities, my cheeks were the color of Mother's flaming red lipstick. She just stood there and let him. He said he found nothing wrong with me, but I knew there was now. I had been violated. Humiliated, I was happy to go home.

I learned to try very hard to keep my ailments to myself.

Chapter 17
Back to Reality

"Jo!" Jacob startled me away from my daydreaming.

"Sorry," I said. "I just can't remember much about three days ago."

"You said Blackie greeted you with bloody footprints." Jacob tried to bring me into the immediate past.

"Let me think. Yes. It was really strange that Blackie was in the house. I had coffee for me and Dad. I set it down on the entry table and kneeled down to check Blackie's feet. I got blood on my hands. I thought he had cut his foot on something. I called out for Dad and got no answer. Blackie was whining, so I took him to the kitchen sink to get a rag and washed his feet. His feet were okay."

"Then what did you do?" Jacob asked.

"I looked around and saw the footprints went through the kitchen, through the dining room, then saw they went up and down the stairs." I was struggling to remember that early morning. "I called out for Dad again," I continued.

"Did you go upstairs?" asked Jacob.

"Blackie did. He ran right up there and stood at the landing, barking at me. He was barking at me to come up. I hate the upstairs in that house. I don't have a room there anymore. Thank God. My room turned into the junk room. Jessie's room is now a library to accommodate Mother's voracious thirst for reading fiction, especially pornographic romance. I very rarely ever went in my parent's room. It was usually locked. It was the only door in the whole house that was ever locked."

"Why do you think it was locked?" Jacob asked.

"Well, to keep the kids out, I guess. I know they used to hide things in there."

"Things?" questioned Jacob.

"Guns. Dad loves to hunt for his food once in a while, and he keeps his guns in the closet in there. And dirty books. Mother is addicted to them. And presents." I was thinking.

"Presents?" he asked.

"Yes, Mother loved to shop for small gifts for every occasion, and she kept a supply on hand for any event—birthdays, new-born babies, anniversaries, Christmas. She couldn't go anywhere without bringing a small gift. She used red wrapping paper for every present."

Red-wrapped presents… My mind pulled me there to escape thinking about my present situation.

CHAPTER 18
THE RED GIFT

It pulled me back to Mother's birthday in early December. I was old enough to know I wanted to get her my own present, pick it out myself, and spend my own money. I wanted to try real hard to please her. The day before the celebration, Dad took Jessie, Johnny, and me to Salet's Department Store in Owatonna to shop for her. He very rarely took Jimmy anywhere with us because he was a baby for so long.

There were no exciting stores in Havana. There were two small food marts. One was dirtier than the other. The owners were related to each other, and the competition was fierce as more and more people were driving cars and going up to the big town where things were a bit fresher, cleaner, and cheaper. There was the Larson Hardware Store with a few pretty knickknacks in the window, but children were scared to go in there because the owner yelled at them.

We all loved going up to the big town of Owatonna, which had a population of a whopping eleven thousand, compared to the smallness of Havana, with only seven hundred residents. It was just a few miles up the highway.

Tightly in my hand, I held onto the money I had been saving. In Salet's, we slowly made our way up and down the aisles, looking at the money in our hands and the prices of the things that caught our eyes. Jessie stopped at the jewelry counter where she and Johnny figured they could each afford one pretty red glass earring to get her the pair. It was quite an ingenious way for Johnny to get the same thing as Jessie.

When I came upon the craft aisle of the toy section, my interest was aroused. There was a red metal loom with a bag of multicolored loops to make pot holders. That looked like I could do it myself and looked like so much fun too. With Dad's approval of our gifts, we checked out.

In the car, Jessie belittled my idea. When she and Johnny showed off the sparkling red glass earrings, I had second thoughts about my gift.

After supper that evening, I excitedly retreated to my bedroom to make the potholders. I had so much fun stretching and crisscrossing the loops through the loom. When I had used up all the loops, I had made five potholders. I used all the red loops first to make two for mother, knowing red was her favorite color. I made the other three multicolored, minus the red loop.

I felt proud that I made them myself. I wrapped them up for the party and saved the other three to give one to Grandmother Lewis and two to give Henrietta gifts for Christmas.

Friday evening, Jessie, Johnny, and I waited with much anticipation to get supper over with so Mother could open her gifts. Grandmother Lewis had made a cake. It was German chocolate. I knew Mother didn't care for the German chocolate flavor, and that is probably why Grandmother Lewis made it just for her.

"The Germans are too cheap to put enough chocolate in it to be good," was what she had said after the last time Grandmother Lewis had brought one over. As soon as we had sung the traditional Happy Birthday Song, Johnny and Jessie thrust their gifts at Mother, insisting she open theirs first. She did.

"Oh, what a beautiful earring!" she exclaimed to Johnny. She put it right on her ear, and I thought it was beautiful.

"Oh, what another beautiful earring!" she exclaimed to Jessie. She put it right on her other ear, and I thought that one was beautiful too. Jessie and Johnny beamed with delight as the family enjoyed mother enjoying her earrings.

My gift was next. I could hardly wait until she got the wrapping off.

Before she could speak, I offered, "I made them all by myself."

"Did you, Jo? Oh how nice," Mother said in a deadpan voice as she pushed them aside.

I knew the difference in the voice and in the face. My countenance sunk like a defeated battleship.

Just fourteen days later was the last day of school before Christmas vacation. As I was eating breakfast, I noticed three small presents wrapped in bright red shiny Christmas paper sitting in the middle of the kitchen table. I also noticed just before Jessie and Johnny left for school, they each grabbed one of the gifts and went out the door. As I was getting suited and booted up for the five-block walk to school, Mother handed me one of the presents. Dumbly, I wondered what I had done to deserve it. I knew there were a few more days to go before Christmas.

"Give this to Mrs. Lovdahl today. It is her Christmas present from you," she said.

"From me?" I personally had no intention of blessing Mrs. Lovdhal. I looked at the tag, and it read, "To Mrs. Lovdahl - From Jo Lewis."

"But I don't want to give her a present," I responded and gave it back to Mother. "You give it to her."

"I don't care what you want. It is expected behavior to give your teacher a gift," she said, pushing the present back at me.

"No, I won't give her a present. I don't like her," I responded, shoving the gift back in her hand. I was not about to reward Mrs. Lovdahl for being mean to me.

"Yes, you will take it and be nice to her," said Mother. "Or you will get a spanking."

"Then spank me now and let me go because I won't give her a present," I said indignantly.

Sandra had no patience at all today. "Why you little spoiled brat," she said. "I will spank you now and then you will give the present to your teacher too."

How could I be spoiled? I wondered. *Can you get spoiled from being unloved and spanked every day?*

She grabbed me by the arm and pulled me over her lap and began thrashing me. It didn't hurt so badly because I already had my snow pants on, but I cried out loudly so she would think I was in pain and would then stop beating on me.

"There!" barked Mother. "I hope you are happy now. Take the present to Mrs. Lovdahl or there will be more of that waiting for you when you get home." She seemed to be grinding her teeth and hissing.

A poison snake face, I thought. *I had better back away. If she bites me I might die.* Pouting, I took the gift and trudged out the door. *Another spanking*, I considered. *That wouldn't be so bad.* Through the snow I plodded, wondering what stupid thing was inside the beautiful red wrapping. Into the school and straight into the coatroom I went. My dislike for Mrs. Lovdahl was boiling into hatred. After all, it was her fault I got spanked already today.

By now, I had had lots of practice donning and doffing the red Shirley Temple costume. I was now able to get the snow pants off before the second bell rang. I had determined I would withhold the gift. I would make my own choices, good or bad, and take the punishment, deserved or not. I hid Mrs. Lovdahl's present inside the deplorable snow pants and hung them up. I guess they were good for something after all. Into the room I marched, feeling superior to everyone in the classroom. I wasn't sure how I could be so superior when I was such a spoiled brat.

Mrs. Lovdahl was sitting at her desk, waiting for all the children to arrive. Every single one of them except for me dutifully walked over to her and hugged her and gave her a gift, which she put on her desk in a neat pile, happily declaring she would open them all after lunch at our Christmas party.

After lunch, Mrs. Lovdahl did just as promised. She set out snacks for us—decorated Christmas cookies, fruit punch, and popcorn. All three were favorite foods of mine. There was no milk to force down my throat.

Hmm, not a bad party, I mused.

After we had played a few games, sang a few songs, and ate a few snacks, Mrs. Lovdahl sat at her desk and began to open her presents. One by one, she appropriately handed out thanksgivings to the donor of each gift. There were knickknacks, books, foodstuffs, coffee mugs, specialty teas, and a bunch of other pretty useless things. She was being so nice to everyone. My resolve was beginning to waver.

When she picked up the last gift that was on her desk, I decided I had better go and get my present. My feelings were warming up a little. I went out to the coatroom. I dug the present out of the hiding spot and brought it into the classroom. As I marched up to Mrs. Lovdhal, she looked at me and frowned. Looking at her face gave me a chill. My feelings began to change back rapidly so I threw the present on her desk.

"Here," I loudly proclaimed. "I didn't want to give it to you, but my mother made me."

Mrs. Lovdahl responded in a way I never expected. She began to cry and left the room without saying a word.

What a big baby, I thought. I looked around at all the surprised kids. *Yep, big baby teacher for a bunch of big babies.*

All the kids remained silent and still until, after a quite a few minutes, Mrs. Lovdahl came back to the classroom. She was composed now, and before long, the day was over. She did not thank me for the present or even open it.

I got myself suited and booted up in record time, and as I trudged home through the snow, I wondered just what was in the beautifully wrapped red gift.

When I got home, Mother was in the kitchen leaning against the counter with arms folded across her chest, and she seemed very annoyed. Her foot was tapping, and she was biting her red-painted lower lip. Uh-oh. I got that icky feeling creeping in my gut. Amazing how my body can tip me off to what is coming next.

"I got a another call today from the school," mother began. "I thought you were done embarrassing me."

Me, embarrass you? I thought incredulously.

"Apparently," she continued, "you said something mean to Mrs. Lovdahl and made her cry."

"She's a tattletale. You said nobody likes a tattletale," I said, desperately trying to find a motive for my actions. Looking at her face, I knew she thought it was a lame excuse.

"That is unacceptable behavior, Jo Lewis." She said my name as if it was poison. "When Christmas vacation is over, the very first thing you will do is apologize to Mrs. Lovdahl."

Mother did not say anymore while she watched me disrobe my Shirley Temple outfit. I was really uncomfortable, feeling her angry eyes staring at me. Then, of course, she calmly picked up the yardstick from off the counter where she had already laid it, waiting just for me. She grabbed my arm and spanked me until the stick broke from the strength of her fury.

"Now get out of my sight!" she hollered as she shoved me to the other room.

The only thought that came to my mind was, *I wonder what the gift was?*

The day before Christmas, I wrapped up the two potholders I made for Henrietta. I took them over to her house and knocked on the door.

"Why, Merry Christmas, Jo. Come right on in." Henrietta was so happy to see me. She grabbed my hand and pulled me in the door.

"Merry Christmas," I said, grinning from ear to ear. She always made me feel so special no matter what. I handed her the gift.

"For me?" she asked gleefully. I nodded. "I love presents," she said as she tore the paper off. "Oh, how wonderful. Why, Jo, thank you so much, my little darling." She hugged me and kissed me, and it seemed to me like it must have been the best present she had ever received. "Come," she said, dragging me into the kitchen. "I have the perfect spot for them right by the stove."

There were two potholders hanging on a hook right by the stove. Henrietta took them off and put the ones I had made for her in their place. "There, right where I can see them every single day and remember how much I love my little Jo," said Henrietta, stepping back to get a good view of the potholders. "Beautiful. They are just beautiful. Thank you so much, Jo," she said.

We ate cookies and drank juice together. She knew I did not like milk. I went home and looked around the kitchen for the potholders I had made for Mother's birthday. They were nowhere to be seen.

RED

The rest of Christmas vacation seemed to drag. Santa had brought everybody except me what they had asked for. Yes, It's true. I couldn't believe it. Jessie wanted a bike, and she got one. It was beautiful, with no crossbar, just for a girl. It was a shiny red-and-white-colored 20" Schwinn, just her size. She would have to wait to ride it though, but I knew when the snow was gone, she would be showing it off all over town. Of course, immediately, I was forbidden to touch it. Johnny, who couldn't think for himself, had wanted a bike too. He got a gleaming green-and-white-colored 20" Schwinn boy's bike, just his size. Jimmy, who wanted a "horth," got a beautiful white wooden rocking horse. I spotted it under his stocking and thought it would go well with the guns that were coming my way. I wanted double-holstered, cast iron, cowboy cap guns if I couldn't have a monkey. No such luck. I got a baby doll. Sadly disappointed, I tried out the rocking horse, hoping it would make me feel better.

"No! Mine horth," Jimmy pulled at me, trying to dismount me. He was no match for this cowboy, I thought. I kicked him away. "Mama!" he ran screaming into the kitchen. I ignored him, riding faster. No one could catch this cowboy now.

"Jo!" shrieked Mother. "Get off Jimmy's horse, and don't you ever ride it again. You are way too big."

I brought "White Lightning," the name I had secretly given the horse, to a halt and jumped off. Jimmy climbed on and rode away, leaving me standing there, daydreaming.

Too big? I recalled hearing it before. Even though I was three years older than Jimmy, I wasn't much bigger than he was. He was tall and heavy for his age, and I was just the opposite—short and light.

When Christmas vacation was over, I dreaded going back to school knowing I would be forced to repent and face Mrs. Lovdahl. The day did come however. I was hoping Mother had forgotten all about the red gift, and I could be free of shame without incident. Not a chance.

As I was leaving for school that morning, Mother said, "Do not come home until you have apologized."

"To who?" I acted as if I didn't remember.

"Mrs. Lovdahl," Mother said.

"For what?" I acted surprised, as if I still didn't remember.

"Jooooo." Mother swallowed hard after saying my name as if speaking it out would cause her to heave out a demon. Her eyes were reflecting red in the pupils. Was I imagining it? The corners of her mouth turned down. Her bright red lower lip began to quiver. "I mean it," she said harshly in a deep, slow, growling whisper. It sent a chill down my spine, and I backed down like a dog with its tail between its legs. I shivered even though I was suited and booted up already.

I caved. Nothing more needed to be said by either one of us.

In the coatroom, as they were disrobing the cumbersome outerwear, the kids were showing off their new clothes to each other. It seemed Christmas had been fruitful for most of them. I did not have anything new to show to anyone.

When I walked into the room, I searched around for the presents the children had given Mrs. Lovdahl. I saw none of them in the room. She must have taken them all home. I also did not see the unwrapped red gift I had thrown on her desk.

All day, the clock ticked by slowly, the slowest I had ever seen. Would this day ever end? With every opportunity I had to repent, procrastination took over instead. Finally, the last bell rang, and I took my time about getting suited and booted up for the walk home. At last, every other child had left the vicinity. I literally inched my way back into the room and over to Mrs. Lovdahl's desk where she was sitting and looking down at some papers, obviously pretending not to notice me. How could she not; this Shirley Temple ensemble was a neon sign.

"Teacher," I addressed her.

"What, Jo?" she said it without looking up. She knew it was me.

"I'm sorry," I ventured, giving as little as I possibly could.

"For what?" She wanted more.

"For throwing your present on your desk," I added.

"Okay," she said without feeling behind it.

I backed up three steps and turned toward the door. I felt like I had done my duty, but I still had to know what was in the gift. I turned back toward Mrs. Lovdahl.

"I have a question," I braved.

"What is it?" she asked, finally glancing up at me with her eyes but not her head.

"What was the gift I gave you?" Courageous words at last.

"You mean the one you threw on my desk?" Was she trying to humiliate me more?

"Yes," I said.

"There were two small red potholders. I thought you made them for me," she said as she leaned back in her chair and looked me square in the eyes.

"I…I…I…did make them," I stammered. My heart was beginning to race at the realization, and even though I tried to stop it, tears began escaping from my eyes. I turned away and ran out.

"They were very nice, Jo. Thank you!" Mrs. Lovdahl hollered after me.

If reincarnation were true, I'd ask to come back as my mother's mother.

Chapter 19

Promises

"Jo. Stay with me here. Did you go upstairs, Jo?" Jacobs voice was stern. I found myself staring at his red necktie.

What an awful color, I thought. "Did I go upstairs that day? I'm thinking," I said, tapping my fingers on the table.

*****

I began thinking about a different set of stairs to avoid thinking about the bloody stairs in the big house. They were the stairs in the front of the church sanctuary that stepped up to the altar. There were only four beautiful stone steps that went all the way across the front of the stone platform.

I recalled part of a Bible verse: "The Lord make his face shine on you and be gracious to you."[6] Yes, shine on me God. Lord, I need you.

It gave me some comfort and brought memories of my confirmation when I was thirteen years old. I was standing outside in the morning sunshine in my new white dress—a sleek pure white, fitted shift dress that landed an inch above my knees.

Henrietta had taught me how to sew, and she often gave me pieces of fabric so it didn't cost me much to just buy a zipper or some buttons. I sewed most of my own clothes from the time I was only nine years old. I had made this dress just the day before. It was very

---

[6] Numbers 6:25 (NIV)

Jackie Kennedy in style. She was the wife of our beloved president, and I loved her chic clothing style, only shorter for me.

Mother was always adamant that our dresses were to the knees in a proper modest fashion. To keep from always arguing about the length, I kept a roll of masking tape in my locker at school and one in Robert's car. That way, I could leave the house in proper fashion and then turn the hemline up with tape, in proper Twiggy style once I got out the house. I never once forgot to rip the tape out before I went home.

I chuckled to myself, thinking of a picture in my yearbook. It was the sophomore class choir photo. Because I was short, I was always in the front row. There I stood with my plaid skirt obviously four inches shorter than anyone else's. Thank God Mother never wanted to look at the book.

Dad took a picture of me before we left for the church. I didn't mind having to dress proper for church.

As soon as I walked in to the children's chapel/dining hall where our white gowns were waiting for us, Robert sauntered up to me and looked me up and down with that great big grin that I loved so much. He looked so clean with his fresh haircut and new shoes peeking out from under his white gown.

"Looks like someone wants to get married, all dressed in white," he teased.

"Well, looks like you want to get married too," I teased back.

He grabbed a hymnbook that was on the table close by and flipped it open to the marriage ceremony. Robert jumped up on a step that was behind him.

"Dearly beloved," he said. "I do. Whom therefore God has joined together, let no one put asunder." He shut the book and put it back on the table. "Now, Robert, you may kiss your bride."

As he stepped down and reached out for me, I backed away laughing and found my gown. I was looking forward to marrying him one day, but today, I was looking forward to knowing the peace that passes all understanding.

During the ceremony, we stepped up four steps to the railing. In my stair-counting obsession, I counted them as I went—one, two, three, four—and knelt down before the altar.

When my turn came, the pastor placed his hand on my head and said, "The Lord bless you and keep you; the Lord make his face shine upon you and be gracious to you; the Lord turn his face toward you and give you peace."[7] The church bell rang three times and I felt a surge of fire within, deep down in my heart and soul. It caused a flood of emotion in me, which I didn't completely discern. It made me cry. I tried hard to not let anyone see I was crying.

"Stop crying, or I'll give you something to cry about," was what Mother said no matter who was crying for any reason. Thankfully, she was not in attendance. She didn't like Dad's church. She did read her Bible, but she seemed to have a twisted theology—her own severe take on everything.

*****

"Jo, did you go up the stairs?" Jacob's voice jolted me back to the present. He was struggling to get me to remember.

"I called up the stairs for Dad because Blackie was barking." I was trying to recall.

"Did you go upstairs?" Jacob asked again.

"There are sixteen stairs. I always count them when I run up. I never walk up because I am scared to look out the window of the landing when it is dark. One, two, three, four, five, six, seven, eight, nine, ten, then turn on the landing, eleven is the next landing, and twelve, thirteen, fourteen, fifteen, and sixteen is the top." As I said it, I knew it was irrational. It felt like danger was coming.

"Did you go up those stairs that day, Jo?" Jacob asked. He was beginning to wonder if he would ever get an answer to that question.

"Yes, I did. I ran up them, counting as I went." I shut my eyes and watched my self run up those stairs.

"Then what, Jo? What did you see? What did you do?" Jacob asked.

---

[7] Numbers 6:24–26 (NIV)

"I saw their bedroom door was open." I began shaking violently as I was beginning to remember. I felt like I was freezing.

"It's okay, Jo," said Jacob as he got up and took the blanket from my cot. He wrapped it around my shoulders. I began sobbing like I have never cried before. "It's okay, Jo. I promise," he said.

I must have cried several minutes.

"Promise?" I questioned Jacob.

"I promise," he promised.

As I gathered my composure, I looked at his face for the first time. He looked old enough to be a grandfather, but he did not have that old weathered farmer look I was accustomed to. He had nice grey eyes that went well with his grey hair at the temples.

"Who is paying you to defend me?" I asked. "I don't have much money."

"Well, I am a court-appointed lawyer since you were unable to request a lawyer of your choice when you were arrested," he answered.

"Yeah, I don't remember," I said.

"I know," he said.

"If you don't win, what will happen to me?" I asked him.

Jacob sighed deeply. "There are quite a few variables here, Jo. That will all depend on what our final decision for your defense is. It could be temporary insanity. It could be self-defense. It could be just plain not guilty. Then there is the point of premeditation. Did you plan the murder? Was it an accident? Other factors involved would be the evidence, the testimony of witnesses, the jury, the judge… At this point, there is no way of knowing the end result for sure."

"Have you ever defended a murderer before?" I asked.

"No. There has never been a murder in Owatonna or Havana for as long as I can remember. You have generated a lot of publicity in the area," said Jacob. "I promise to do the best job I possibly can. In my heart, I believe everything is going to be all right." I think he felt a deep-seated need to give me hope.

"Promises," I sighed. "Mother never promised anything but punishment for bad behavior. And there was never a reward for good behavior. Dad always keeps his promises. Robert gave me a promise ring. See. I never take it off."

I lifted my hand to show Jacob the gold ring that spelled "LOVE," using a heart for the letter *O*, and in the middle of the heart was a diamond. I gasped when I looked at my bare hand. There was no ring.

"I'm sorry," said Jacob. "I am sure it is lovely. No prisoner is allowed to wear jewelry in here."

*****

I rubbed my ring finger where the ring was supposed to be and remembered the night Robert gave it to me. It was the night of his graduation from high school, one year ahead of me. Robert's mother worked at a Ford dealership, and for graduation, he got a new car. It was a 1967 Ford Fairlane GT. It was a silver two-door hardtop with bench seats and four on the floor. All his buddies mocked him out for the bench seats. After all, bucket seats were all the modern rage for real men, but he loved the bench so I could sit really close to him in the car.

"It's the best feature!" he would laughingly tell all the guys.

When the party was over, we drove it out into the countryside and found a sweet spot in a cornfield to make out. After a few long and warm kisses, he reached under the front seat and pulled out a small ring box.

"Jo," he said as he handed me the box. "Will you marry me when I get home from the army?"

"You know I will, Robo," I said. Then, teasingly, I grabbed the box and threw it into the back seat. "Or maybe not," I said, laughing. He climbed back there to get it, and I climbed right on top of him.

"Promise," he said as he put the ring on my finger.

"Promise," I said.

We both felt that sweet contentment of love. We made out until the dreaded curfew hour crept in on us. The curfew really irritated Robert because he didn't have one, but he always took me home on time.

"This is my house," said Mother in that bossy haughty voice of hers. "When Jo lives here, she will obey my rules," is what she told Robert when he asked permission to have me out later than curfew. He was afraid of the wrath of Mother, just like everybody else.

CHAPTER 20
THE RED TAIL

Dad promised he would buy me a red-tailed monkey. He loved to talk about the monkey. He said it was a *Cercopithecus ascanius*. He loved saying the strange and intelligent-sounding words. He said they lived in the rainforest of Uganda, Africa, but he was going to find me one.

Mother said he would never get me one because monkeys stink, and she would not allow that in her house.

"The red-tailed monkey likes to eat all day long. He has pouches in his cheeks. He can store the food in there and save it for later," Dad explained.

"What does he eat?" I wanted to know.

"He stuffs his cheeks with fruit, vegetables, nuts, eggs, sugar cane, and *posho*."

"What is *posho*?" I asked.

"I don't know," said Dad. "But they like it. They eat flowers too."

"That must be why the red-tailed monkey saved the little girl." I said.

"Why?" asked Dad.

"Because she was picking flowers for him to eat," I responded.

"Good idea," said Dad. "They like to eat grasshoppers and ants too," he added.

"Icky," I giggled. "Do they like bread and butter?"

"I'm sure they do," said Dad.

"Me too," I said.

"I know," said Dad, giving me a little squeeze. "Did you know they take a nap in the middle of the day?" asked Dad.

"No, I didn't," I responded.

"They like it, and they don't fuss about it," said Dad, smiling.

I thought if the beloved red-tailed monkey could take a nap without a fuss, maybe I could try not to fuss next time.

"The best part is the kiss," said Dad.

"Why?" I asked. Of course, I wanted to know the best part.

"They do the red-tail monkey kiss just like this." Dad took my face in his hands and put his nose down to mine and rubbed my nose with his.

"I like the red-tailed monkey kiss," I said.

"Me too," said Dad.

I love monkeys. Ever since I can remember, I had wanted one for a pet. The spring that I was six, my dad took me to the dime store in a different town where he had been fishing on the lake. I was usually willingly go fishing with him, and it was his favorite pasttime. We watched a monkey in a cage that was for sale. I was thrilled with the possibility.

"Can we get it?" I pleaded.

"They're a lot of trouble," Dad said, trying to discourage me. I begged and begged for the monkey.

"Your mother says they stink." He tried to dissuade me.

"We can give him a bath," I offered with hope.

"They are messy eaters and throw their food all over the floor," Dad said.

"I will clean it up every day." I was convinced I could handle it.

I know Dad thought about it, and I'm sure I had him almost persuaded until the store clerk said, "He bites."

"Oh no," said Dad, shaking his head. "I can't let my little Jo be bitten by a monkey."

And you are a jerk, I said to the clerk in my mind.

We left the store, but Dad promised me he would buy me a red-tailed monkey for my birthday. I believed him.

Every night from then on, when I said my prayers, I would secretly add, "And please, dear Jesus, I need a monkey."

The seventh birthday came in mid-May. I had already told everybody in school I was going to get a red-tailed monkey for my birthday. I had no doubt because Dad had actually said he would get me a monkey.

George Skogstad, who sat next to me in school, said, "I don't believe you." He thought he knew everything.

My second-grade teacher, Mrs. Gravely, said, "That's nice," as she rolled her eyes and walked away.

It was Saturday, and my seventh birthday was a very exciting day—a very long day because of the anticipation. After supper was celebration time with the birthday cake. I sheepishly looked at everyone's faces while they sang Happy Birthday. Of course, Jessie and Johnny made faces at me while they sang. I made my wish for the monkey and blew out the seven candles of the marshmallow-frosted chocolate fudge double-layer cake. Thankfully, Grandmother Lewis didn't make this one. This is the only trait I figured I had inherited from my mother—a love for chocolate.

I didn't see any presents on the table, but I was happy. And then there he was, just as promised. Dad just handed him to me and said, "Here's your red-tailed monkey, Jo. I had him wrapped up, but he already ripped the paper off. He's a little monkey all right."

Yes, there he finally was, my only gift that day. The cutest monkey I had ever seen, and no trouble at all. He never bit me. He instantly became my best friend, traveling companion, and bed partner. It was love at first sight. I was a believer in love at first sight. It was that way the first time I saw Robert.

"He doesn't have a tail, Dad," I commented, wondering why not.

"Well, red-tailed monkeys don't have tails when they are born. I thought you knew that," said Dad.

"Will it grow?" I asked.

"No, it won't grow, but we will have one surgically attached tomorrow," said Dad.

"Okay," I said. "What's his name?"

"He doesn't have a name yet. You will have to name him," said Dad.

"Nadahunga!" I shouted out. "His name is Nadahunga."

Nadahunga was a chimpanzee, but I did not know the difference. He was a monkey, and that was all I cared about.

A little later that evening, Jessie and Johnny sauntered over to me.

"Can we see your monkey?" Jessie asked for both her and Johnny.

With some concern, I held him up for them to see.

"Can we hold him?" Jessie asked. I felt uneasy. They were never nice to me. I pulled Naduhunga in close to my body.

"No," I said. Simultaneously, they reached out to grab the monkey. Johnny knocked him out of my arms, and Jessie snatched him up and ran. Johnny followed close at her heels. They ran upstairs and into Jessie's room where they shut the door and held it shut. I raced after them. Their hilarious laughter was drowned out by my screaming. I began kicking the bedroom door.

"Dad!" I screamed. "Help me! Dad!" He couldn't hear me. He was outside mowing the lawn.

Mother did hear me though. "Stop that screaming, Jo, before I give you something to scream about!" she shouted up the stairs at me.

"Jessie and Johnny took my monkey and won't give him back," I was sobbing.

Mother started up the steps. It made me uncomfortable hearing her foot slam down on each step. I counted her steps. As she rounded the top banister, I could see she had a stick in her hand. All of a sudden, I was stricken with terror, and my body began to shake uncontrollably. I cowered away from her and sat down on the other side of the hallway. Still shaking, my eyes closed and tightened, my chin went down to my chest, my hands clenched into fists, and my arms went instinctively up to a defensive position crossing above my head.

"That's what I thought," Mother said. "I'll kick you into the middle of next week if you don't shut your mouth." She turned around and went back down the stairs.

I was bewildered. I was spared a thrashing, but I still did not have my monkey. In the quiet of the house now, I could hear the lawn mower still roaring outside. Then I heard Jessie and Johnny laughing again. Jessie's bedroom door opened up, and Nadahunga was heartlessly thrown out into the hall. With relief, I jumped up and grabbed him. I ran into my room and hopped up onto my own bed. I held Nadahunga tightly until I had calmed down. After I relaxed and felt safe again, I took a good look at the monkey to see if he was okay. My countenance fell when I realized what they had done to him. "STUPID" was written in ink, right across his plastic nose.

No use to tell Mother. I was sure she would not care. Dad was still mowing. I thought maybe I could wash it off so I trekked to the bathroom, got a wet washrag and some soap, and scrubbed away. I scrubbed hard. It was still there but a little faded. Next, I took Nadahunga downstairs to the kitchen. Under the sink I found the Comet Cleanser. I tried again, scrubbing and scrubbing. It was faint now, but I could still see it. Dad eventually finished mowing and came into wash up, but I decided not to tell him.

I did not mind going to bed that night. In fact, I simply put myself to bed. I wanted to get away from everyone else and just find comfort in Nadahunga. It was barely getting dusky outside as I lay there in my bed, examining Nadahunga. He was so cute with his happy plastic face, a smile frozen in time. No matter what my mood was, his would never change. His eyes and eyelids were powder blue with gleaming black pupils.

It sort of looks like make up, I thought. He had the roundest little puffy cheeks and a bright red, slightly open mouth. *His lipstick is just like Mother's*, I thought incredulously. *That might not be good.*

His plastic ears come straight off his face, out the sides of his head. His plastic hands and feet looked just like people feet to me. All of his soft and fuzzy fur was black except for his chest and back. They were bright yellow.

"Nadahunga, I love you," I whispered to him. He smiled back at me.

When I was old enough to think about kissing a boy, I would practice kissing his ears. I was sure the way my lips fit so comfortably in the curves of his ear would be about the way it would feel to kiss a boy.

I knew my older sister Jessie had kissed boys already. Seriously, I asked her to try it and tell me if it was so. Seriously, she did and said, "Yes, it feels something like that." I was riddled with the giggles that she kissed the monkey's ear.

"It looks like I made a monkey out of her," I laughed.

The next day was Sunday, and I tried to bring Nadahunga to church. I did not want to leave him out of my sight for fear that someone else might do something else bad to him. All my pleading fell on deaf ears so I stuffed him in the bottom drawer of my dresser, thinking he would be safe there. He was.

After lunch, just as promised, Dad took me to Mrs. Harleigh's house where he said Nadahunga was to get his tail surgery. She was an old neighbor lady whom Dad looked out for. He mowed her lawn and shoveled her driveway even though she did not have a car. Mrs. Harleigh sewed corduroy mittens and hand puppets and sold them at her "summer-long" garage sale.

When we stepped inside Mrs. Harleigh's house, I wondered if she was a doctor too.

"Well then, Jo, let me see the patient," she said. I willingly handed him over.

She looked him over and said, "Hm, it is just as you have said, James. This poor red-tailed monkey does not have his tail. I have just what he needs. She sat down on a chair at the table and picked up a red fuzzy tail that she had previously made just for Nadahunga. Nimbly, and quickly for an old woman, she sewed the tail right on Nadahunga in the right spot. It was perfect.

Not many things are perfect, but that was.

Chapter 21
Robert Hoffman

I think Jacob was getting weary of me drifting off into my own thoughts. I was weary of trying to remember the murder of my mother.

"Jo," he said. "I need to go get a cup of coffee. Should I bring one back for you?"

"Sure, with cream and sugar please," I said, looking forward to the pick-me-up.

Alone again in my cell. the same questions began to flood my mind. *How long will this dreadful routine go on? Why am I here? Where is my dad? Why can't I remember recent events?*

After he left, I sat on the floor and leaned up against the door so I could sit in the morning sunshine. Regrettably, it was a cloudy day, but thinking about Robert and his green eyes encouraged me, even better than the sun.

About the same time Nadahunga came into my life, Robert Hoffman came on the scene too. These two made my life bearable.

Mother was strict about dating, and I always had to fight to see Robert as much as I could. He held the title to all my firsts. He was the first to smile at me. I was only in the first grade, but the impression it made on me would last a lifetime. No other smile from any other boy anywhere would compare. It cheered my very soul.

He was the first to hold my hand. I was in seventh grade. An assembly was being held in the gymnasium at the end of the school day. I walked in with Martine, and we sat a couple of rows up in the bleachers. The haughty seniors and juniors would never let the underclassmen sit near the top. If we ever dared, we would be teased and humiliated until we descended. Robert had watched for me to come, and as soon as I sat down, he rushed to my left side and sat right next to me. I was so proud. Martine did not have a boyfriend, so I felt a little puffed up. After a couple of minutes of feeling the rush of being loved, he put his right hand palm up on my lap, and I put my left hand right into his, entwining our fingers together—a perfect fit. Even if I tried, I could never forget the rush it gave me.

That day after school, I stopped at Henrietta's house before going home. She was easy to talk to about boys and pretty much about anything really. That day, I needed advice. If I ever asked Mother any questions about boys, she would just yell at me that I was not old enough to think about them.

I stopped at the door of her house and picked a daisy. Then I knocked.

"Come in!" sang out Henrietta.

I went in and closed the door. "Henrietta?" I called out to her. She came waltzing into the kitchen.

"Hello, little Jo," she greeted me, singing my name. "Rough day?" she asked, smiling.

"Nothing that a cookie couldn't cure," I said, hinting for one.

"Come on then, and have a seat," she said. I sat at the table and then quick as a wink, there appeared a cookie and a glass of juice in front of me.

"Henrietta?" I began.

"Yes, love," she responded.

"How do you know if a boy loves you for sure or not?" I asked.

"Well, you have the test right there in your hand," she said.

"Which one?" I asked. "The cookie or the daisy?"

"Why, the daisy of course." She took the daisy and pulled a petal off.

"He loves me," she said. Then she pulled another one off and said, "He loves me not." She handed me back the flower. "Now you pull them all off and see what the last petal says."

"He loves me. He loves me not," I repeated over and over again as I pulled each petal off until there was only one left. "He loves me," I said with a smile.

"See," said Henrietta. "The daisies never lie. They always say I love you."

I was a pretty good math student. I knew it was a coincidence, and I didn't really need the confirmation. I knew Robert loved me even if Mother insisted it was just a passing crush.

He was the first to kiss me. Does anyone ever forget their first kiss?

Mine was a dusky summer evening. Robert and I had spent the afternoon at the carnival in the school yard, mostly just walking around. I was warned to be home before dark. When the sun was going down, we slowly walked hand in hand to the big house, both wishing the night would never end. We stopped under the elm tree in the front yard. Robert turned to face me, and I bent my face up to meet his. Oh, that grin made me giggle thinking about what I was hoping he would do. The anticipation was heightening our anxiety. It was like a slow motion scene from a movie.

As his face tilted to one side, mine tilted to the other. Our smiles disappeared into desire. Simultaneously, our eyes closed, and in perfect symphony, our lips met and melted into each other's. I was surprised at how his lips felt pressed against mine. They were alive and warm. Move over, Nadahunga. You've got nothing compared to the real thing. His arms went around my body until his hands planted firmly on my back, pulling me in, pressing his chest into mine. My arms went immediately and naturally up around his neck. I had secretly hoped the whole world was watching because I was so happy. We both wanted it to never end. Neither of us moved for fear of losing that perfect feeling of the perfect moment, but alas, the darkness was closing in.

When we finally separated, we were breathless, and both sighed deeply. Then his big beautiful grin came over his face, and I ran to the house, dashed up the five porch steps into the house, and announced to everyone, "He kissed me!"

Jessie and Johnny were sitting at the dining room table, both doing homework. *What a waste of time*, I thought.

Johnny looked up and said, "Roober Goober Boober? That was a big mistake."

Jessie commented without looking up. "Pathetic."

I sang about it and thought about it all night long. "He kissed me. He kissed me. Robby Bobby kissed me."

He was the first to give me a ride in a car. Being the son of a farmer, he had a farmer's permit to drive when he was just fourteen years old. Mother had warned me to never get in a car with a boy. I thought it was a pretty stupid rule.

One sunshiny summer afternoon, Robert drove into town in his dad's flesh-colored convertible. At least that's the color Robert said it was. I say it was pink. It was a day when I just happened to be downtown on main street, getting a Tab out of the Coke machine. He spotted me right away, pulled up to the curb, and stopped. "Hey, Lewis," he flirted. "Want to go for a ride?"

Instinctively, I looked up and looked around to see if there was anyone around who would be able to tell on me. Seeing the coast was clear, I opened the passenger door and hopped in.

"Take me anywhere but home," I said daringly.

Robert set his eyes on the first road out of town and away we went.

"What are you doing way over there?" he asked as soon as we were out of the city limits. He put his right arm up over the back of the seat, inviting me. That was my cue. I took it and scooted over to him as close as I could get. We didn't go far; just a mile or so to the edge of Rice Lake where we parked in a private spot to look at the water. We laughed. We talked. We kissed for an hour until I was uncomfortable, remembering Mother's rules.

So Robert drove me back to the pop machine in town, and I walked home, actually skipping most of the way.

At supper that evening, Mother cleared her throat and looked at me with a frown. "Where were you, Jo, this afternoon?" she asked.

Oofta, I hated her voice. "Just walking around town," I responded.

"Is that all?" she questioned.

"Yes," I lied.

"Carl Johnson called me just before supper and told me he saw you up at the lake in a car with Robert Hoffman. He recognized Robert's dad's car," she flatly accused me.

I felt the blood drain from my face, and I know my cheeks flushed even though my face turned white. "Who is Carl Johnson?" I asked.

"The owner of the property you were parking on," she answered. Ugh, that accusing voice of hers was like fingernails scraping on a blackboard. *What was she going to do about it here at the table? Beat me? Big deal. Robert is worth another beating*, I thought. "How would he know who I was?" I asked.

"We are the Lewises. Everyone knows who I am and who my children are," she said haughtily.

"What's the big deal?" I asked.

"The big deal is you are grounded from everything for three weeks," she responded.

"What does that mean exactly?" I asked. I was raising my voice in distress.

Jessie snickered and kicked Johnny under the table. Johnny snickered and kicked me.

"No TV, no friends, no phone calls, no leaving the yard," she demanded.

"But it is summer," I pleaded. "I have plans. Dad, help me?"

"You know her rules, Shiny," said Dad.

"Oh, poor Sheeny," said Jessie and Johnny in unison, mocking me.

"Why don't you just slap me silly like you always do and get it over with!" I yelled.

"Go to your room!" Mother pushed her chair back and stood up, pointing at the stairwell. "You can come back after we are done eating and do the dishes," Mother growled through clenched teeth. She had no mercy. There was no forgiveness, only her severe justification, just like with every other incident in my life. What a witch.

Why did it seem that every single conversation I had with Mother was an argument over my freedom? I was seething with hatred for her.

*****

Robert was always giving me something. The first thing he ever gave me was a Payday candy bar, and he said, "I love you." One day, after school, cute little green-eyed Robert handed it to me and then dashed off, leaving me smiling. Every time we were together, he left me smiling.

He gave me his car before he left for the army, and I promised to take good care of it. Every month, he sent me one hundred dollars of his paycheck. From a nickel bar to one hundred dollars, the inflation rate seemed to match the inflation rate of our love.

I loved my full-time job working at Salet's Department Store. Now with my paycheck of about forty dollars a week and what Robert sent me, I was able to get an apartment in Owatonna just as soon as I had graduated. I was so excited to get out of Mother's house and be on my own.

CHAPTER 22
THE RED PAJAMAS

Jacob kicked the door with his foot to signal he wanted back in. I heard it and got up. The door opened, and Jacob entered with two coffees. "Here, Jo," Jacob said.

"I am grateful," I said as I took the cup.

"Does Nudahunga still sleep with you?" asked Jacob, chuckling a little at the thought of it.

"He does," I said. "I sure wish I had him here. He has listened to all my trials and joys. He is torn and mended. His fingers are chewed on. But he is still just as comforting as he was when I was only seven. Dad knew what I needed."

We sat at my tiny table and sipped our coffee.

"So getting back to Saturday morning, Jo. You said your parents' bedroom door was open. Did you go in there?" Jacob was pushing me.

"I did," was all I said.

"Can you tell me what you saw and what you did?" asked Jacob.

"I do remember something," was all I could say before I broke down crying again. I wondered how I could cry so much. I was having feelings of desperation.

Jacob gave me a few minutes before he pushed again.

"Jo, you have to tell me every detail so I can defend you."

"I know," I said wearily. "The first thing I noticed was the bed was not made up. It was very unusual. Mother always makes the bed as soon as she gets out of it. There has always been the same quilt on that bed ever since my grandmother died. It is an oversized red and white double wedding ring quilt. My great grandmother made it for my mother. I know Mother picked out the colors. It is all sorts of different patterns of reds. Mother loves the color red. She was close with her grandmother but couldn't stand her own mother who was always sick. Her mother, Edna, kept it from her until she died in 1953. I remember Mother taking it out of the house after the funeral. She said it was the only thing she wanted while her sisters fought over the rest of the stuff. Actually, I was surprised because it was handmade, and Mother dislikes handmade stuff."

I paused.

"An empty unmade bed," I said. "I wondered what was up with that."

I paused again.

"What else did you see, Jo?" Jacob asked.

"Oh my God! There was so much blood on the floor." I closed my eyes. I pressed them shut tightly because I didn't want my mind to see what was next.

"I remember…I saw Mother…lying face down on the floor… with blood all around her." I could barely get the words out.

"Was she naked?" Jacob asked me.

"No," I said, shaking my head from side to side.

"She was wearing red sexy see-through pajamas that looked like what a Bedouin belly dancer would wear. Her midriff was naked though." I rubbed my midriff to show him what I meant. "There were fancy sparkling cuffs at her wrists and ankles." I swallowed hard, feeling nauseated. "I'm gonna be sick." I gulped back the first attempt of my body trying to throw up and quickly crawled over to the toilet, put my head in it, and began heaving.

Jacob gagged and decided to not stick around for the finale.

"I'll come back when you are feeling better, Jo," he said. He called for the door to open, and out he went.

When the nausea ceased, I reached up to the side of my sink where a damp washcloth was resting. I wiped my face and put it back. I couldn't get up so I leaned against the toilet and thought about Mother's red pajamas. I was sure I had seen them somewhere before.

Could it be five years ago? Yes, if memory serves me right.

*****

Jimmy was often sick with swollen tonsils and sore throats. I can't even tell you how many times he had to go on liquid penicillin for it. The one and only time I ever had a sore throat, Jimmy had one too. I bet he gave it to me.

Mother took us both to see Dr. Androvich at the same time. Jimmy was examined first. I recall Dr. Androvich looking in his throat and saying his tonsils were so huge that they were inhibiting his airway, and if he took them out, maybe he would stop having tonsillitis.

When he looked down my throat, all he said was, "Hmmm," and the next thing I knew, Jimmy and I were roommates at the Steele County Hospital in Owatonna, being prepped for a tonsillectomy.

We only stayed one night, and of course, "almost as smart as a doctor," Mother insisted on staying there with us so she could boss the nurses around.

Dr. Androvich seemed to be around a lot. Jimmy got most of the attention. After all, he was the really sick one, and I was probably a "twofer" to keep him company. You know, two for the price of one.

On one of his peek-in visits, Dr. Androvich handed Mother a dress box from Salet's Department Store. I found this very curious. When she left the room for a break, I snuck out of bed and peeked in the box.

When she returned, I asked her what was in the box. She yelled at me that it was none of my business and that I should never mention it again. I didn't. I soon enough forgot about it because I didn't know what it was until today. It was that one and the same belly dancer outfit. I am sure of it even though that was several years ago. My memories stay vivid. The sheer red fabric; the sparkling decorative band that I now know was the waist band. Why would he give her something like that? Why would she be wearing it three days ago, I wondered.

It didn't seem very proper to me.

CHAPTER 23

JESSIE

The hideously loud blat of the speaker woke me up. I had fallen asleep on the floor by the toilet from emotional exhaustion. Hearing the loudspeaker, I realized it was lunchtime, so I quickly got up and stepped out into the line as commanded. As I wondered what crap we were going to get to eat now, I felt the sides of my midriff. I think I was losing weight. I'd probably look pretty good in a belly dancer outfit by now.

"So how did you do it?" whispered #11284774, breaking into my thoughts.

"I bet she slit her throat," whispered #05135776 over her shoulder.

"I bet she strangled her," whispered #11284774. She shoved me.

I began thinking about strangling someone as I followed the line to lunch.

I think I will start with #11284774. I am getting pretty sick of her pushing me, I thought as I pictured my hands around her neck, choking the daylights out of her.

Today, my tray held some kind of nasty bean mash. There was a swirl of creamed spinach and a burnt biscuit with a plop of oleo. I was very hungry now, and it looked like this food might kill me. So kill or be killed. In my mind, I strangled the cook with my foot, stepping on her neck and crushing the life out of her.

I braved a taste. I gagged on my first bite, and #05135776 started snickering. *Now*, I thought. *I will strangle her*. I pictured my hands going around her neck from the back because I didn't want to look at her ugly face. In my mind, I pressed with all my might from the anger of being starved.

I sighed and turned to look at #05135776. *Shoot, she is still there*, I thought. Then, while I was still thinking about strangling her, quick as a wink, she reached over and stole my biscuit. Darn it all anyway! That was the only thing I thought I could possibly eat at this meal.

#11284774 started laughing. *Now I am going to have to strangle her too*, I thought.

I was hungry and I was so mad that I actually found myself back in my cell after lunch thinking it was possible I could have murdered someone.

I remembered the day I had that kind of rage against Jessie.

*****

Jessie was a terrible sister. She belittled me and made fun of me as much as she could. Mother had said I was flat-chested, and big-breasted Jessie loved to expound on that and say I had a disease. That I was puny, underdeveloped, immature, and feeble-minded.

Jessie was the most sophisticated girl in her class, at least she thought so. She always walked with her head high, her nose up in the air, and her shoulders back, which accentuated the line of her well-developed bust. All her clothes were store-bought, just like Mother's. She was fully grown and fully developed in the sixth grade and was very mature minded for a school girl. She was a real snob.

When I first started high school, my feet did not even touch the floor yet when I sat at a desk. *Who cares?* I pondered.

Her boyfriend was three years older than she was. She knew things about necking that none of her friends had even dreamed of yet. She knew secret things that grown-ups did in the bedroom. Once, Jessie and I unsuspectingly opened our parents' bedroom door to find them naked and instantly screaming at us to get out. In shocking surprise, we quickly shut the door.

"Do you think they were doing it?" Jessie asked me.

"Doing what?" I stupidly asked in my innocence.

Shaking her head in disbelief at my immaturity, she just said, "Never mind."

My passion for Nadahunga was more proof to Jessie that I was indeed very immature. Probably went right along with my being underdeveloped.

I don't suspect Jessie had a difficult time growing up in Mother's house. Being highly favored by Mother, she thought she was better than the rest of us. She thought she was cuter and smarter and worked harder. She had no time for me or Jimmy. To her, we were obnoxious brats—a couple of retards.

Because Jessica never accepted me and treated me with disdain, I often thought about strangling her. She was a lot like Mother in that she if she liked the way she did something, then that was the only acceptable way of doing it. She made many remarks that stung me, and she had a queen bee stinger.

After school once, she haughtily said, "Mr. Highlander wants to know when you are going to start living up to the Lewis tradition, which Johnny and I have so superiorly laid down for you, a pathetic peon." It went right along with a song that Mother sang, "Why can't you be more like Jessie."

Mr. Highlander was the social studies teacher. Jessie and Johnny received only *A*s from him, studying earnestly and entering into class discussion with great interest. I managed to pull a *C* without opening the book or my mouth, and I was proud of it.

"Why can't you get your hair ratted up nice and high like mine," she said with snobbery dripping from her lips. I did try, although I personally preferred the softer look.

Once before, I went roller skating. I ratted my hair up with all my might. I thought Jessie would have been truly proud. I snuck into her room to find, of course, the only kind of hair spray a person should use—the tall black aerosol can. Jessie would have screamed at me if she caught me using it. After all, she paid for it herself with her own hard-earned money. I sprayed my bouffant hairdo generously. Then I sprayed it again even more generously for good measure. I looked in her mirror. Wow, just like Jessie's.

RED

Feeling superior, I walked the three blocks to the bus that was waiting to take Havana's eager preteens to the roller skating rink in Owatonna. I held my head high with such *savoir faire*, thinking, *If she could see me now, she would stop making fun of me.*

Just as the bus began turning down the highway to our edifice of fun, Martine greeted me with, "What happened to your hair?"

What indeed. Tonight, I was a Jessite and proud of it.

"It looks wet," she said in a surprisingly disgusted tone.

I reached my hand up there and felt it. The perfect hair had mysteriously fallen flat and felt greasy too. What the ——? I was still too young to say the nasty word out loud, so I just thought it in my mind. Oh no, mortification again—an old familiar feeling. I stole a glance at the back of the bus. Yep, he was there, Robert, grinning at me from ear to ear. I had complete loss of face. If I had only known then Robert would have still liked me even if I shaved my head, I could have spared myself the night of agony.

Whatever had happened? What kind of hairspray was that? I retraced my steps over and over in my mind, trying to figure out where I went wrong. At the roller rink, Martine loaned me her cute little three-cornered scarf, but I still would not come out of the bathroom. What a long night that was. I peeked out once and found Robert skating with some other girl. Oh, the pain of it all. I knew he was too cute to be ignored.

Back in town, I raced home past the schoolyard as fast as I could go. I tore up the sixteen steps, two at a time, and raced into Jessica's room. I grabbed the tall black aerosol can and, to my dismay, found that it was not hairspray. Why hadn't I read the label before? Conditioner? What on earth did she use that for? I finally surmised that because she bleached and ratted so religiously, she had ruined her hair. Taunt or no taunt, I vowed not to copy her ever again.

One night at the supper table, I was sitting across from the stinger bee. Here it comes.

"Jo, when are you ever going to find anyone decent?" To date, she meant.

Robert was the son of a farmer and destined to be one himself. Jessica was dating a college boy destined for high life in the big city. Defiantly, I stood to my feet and screamed at her all the stupid comebacks I could summon up, reviling her beloved boyfriend, Glen, and ran up the stairs.

In her dumbfounded disbelief, she remarked to the others left at the supper table, "What did I say? Such an outrageous outburst, probably due to her being so underdeveloped."

Then one fine day, I know the sun had to be shining this day, when we were both in the upstairs bathroom, she blurted out, "Glen says you would make someone a pretty good wife if you ever got any boobs."

That did it. I couldn't take it any longer. I was almost as tall as she was even though I weighed forty pounds less. Adrenaline began pumping through my angrily-distended veins. I felt the strength of ten men rush into me. I grabbed her like a madman and threw her down right over the edge and into the bathtub. She was quite surprised and immediately got up and out, preparing to put me in my place. I grabbed her again and threw her viciously down on the floor. She felt like a feather to me. She was all looks and no substance after all. She was shocked now, not understanding what spirit from hell had overcome me. She got up again, a little less spirited this time, and I grabbed her and brutally threw her down again and put my foot on her abdomen.

Now her composure was gone. She knew she was bigger and was not about to take any crap from me. She was really angry. She got up and charged me. I was ready for anything she had. I grabbed her and mercilessly threw her down and sat on her holding her wrists to the floor. She lay there in total disbelief, her perfect big-lipped mouth hanging open, all dumbfounded.

"Don't you wish you had full lips like mine instead of those thin ones of yours?" she said, still daring to debase me.

"Look in the mirror, girl. Those lips are fat, not full." That was my victory speech. I jumped up and dusted her germs off my hands. Tentatively, she ventured up one more time just be sure, and I grabbed her and savagely threw her down again. I put my hands around her throat this time wanting to squeeze the life out of her. She pleaded for mercy and conceded defeat. I won, triumphant. Yes, to her surprise, and mine as well, I had won. It really was a fine day after all.

If I couldn't strangle her to death though, how could I kill my mother? Jess was just a little twister; Mother was a tornado.

Chapter 24
The Red Bloody Knife

Jacob was back after lunch and began pushing me again to remember the events of three days ago. He repeated everything back to me that I had said so far. "Is this right, Jo?" he asked.

I nodded.

"You found your mother lying in a pool of blood," he reminded me.

"I did," I said, finally realizing it was reality that my mind couldn't deny. "She was lying in blood. There was with a knife in her back. I couldn't believe my eyes. I just stood there staring at her, trying to evaluate the situation."

"What was your assessment?" he asked.

"The knife sure looks like Dad's knife. I remember thinking to myself, *Dad! What happened? How could you do this?* I know I said that out loud, thinking that I must be in the middle of a bad dream. I could see it plain as day. I didn't want to believe it because of the implications. I recognized the knife. It was a knife Dad loves—a twelve-inch MK2 KA-BAR fighting knife with a six-and-seven-eights-inch blade. He brought it home from the navy after World War II. He used to tell stories about it to the boys."

*****

"See this knife?" Dad said to Johnny and Jimmy. "It is a navy warrior fighting knife. It is used to protect yourself from the enemy. Never take it out of the scabbard unless you intend to use it. When I was on my ship, I always kept it right here on my hip when I was in my uniform, just in case I might need it." Dad patted the spot where he would hook it to the waistband of his bell-bottom sailor pants.

"I never knew when some enemy, like a Japanese fighting soldier, might sneak aboard my ship, and I would have to protect myself," he continued. "I would only plan to use it, Johnny, if I thought someone was going to hurt me. So you can look at it but never touch it." Dad pulled it out from the scabbard and gently touched the sharpened edge. "It is very sharp. It is very dangerous," he said. "It can easily stop the enemy. The enemy, Jimmy, is someone who wants to hurt you."

*****

"I wasn't supposed to hear those stories, but I listened to them anyway. He said he never did have to use it, but if he needed to, he could protect himself in hand-to-hand combat. He had other knives that he took on fishing trips with the boys. They were used to fillet fish. I remember him showing them to Johnny and teaching him how to clean fish with extreme care. He would always sharpen and oil a knife after each use. Jessie and I were never allowed to touch the knives because they was so dangerous."

"Jo," said Jacob. "You saw the knife in your mother's back."

"I did, Jacob," I said. "I knelt right down in the blood. It was sticky. It was terrifying, but I pulled the knife out. I pressed my hand over the hole from the knife. There was no more fresh bleeding. I rolled her over and shook her to wake up. I began yelling for Dad to come and help. He didn't come and she didn't wake up.

"I sat back on my feet and just stared at her face. In life, I couldn't stand what she looked like. Probably because I couldn't stand her. I would have never in a million years said she was good-looking. But looking at her then without a spirit, goodness seemed to be upon her. There was no guile. Nothing cruel or unkind coming forth from her bright red-painted lips. For the first time, I could see why she was beautiful to Dad."

"What did you do with the knife?" Jacob asked.

"I wiped it off on my shirt. I began thinking I needed to protect Dad. I couldn't get it clean so I ran down to the kitchen and washed it in the kitchen sink. I grabbed a kitchen knife that was similar in size and ran back upstairs. I saw the scabbard on the floor not far away and put the cleaned knife back in there. It was Dad's alright. The closet door was open so I put it in Dad's side of the closet next to his gun where he always kept it. I smeared the kitchen knife with blood and laid it in the blood next to her."

I put my head in my hands and sighed.

"They yelled and fought a lot. I thought maybe Mother could kill Dad because I didn't see that she liked him at all, but I never dreamed Dad could kill her because I know he loved her even though I have heard him threaten her."

My memory drifted to just last year...

*****

Mother was sitting at the rarely used kitchen table sipping on a cup of hot tea. That was the only reason I knew it was three thirty in the afternoon—tea time for the English.

I had invited Robert to my senior prom. Fortunately for me, he would be home from boot camp for a week in the spring, and senior prom was scheduled for that very week.

I was voluntarily emptying the dishwasher from the lunch dishes, hoping to soften her up before I asked for forty dollars to buy a store-bought prom dress. I figured, for once, maybe she would like to see me in a store-bought dress.

I had tried it on in Salet's when it first came in and was in love with it. As I twirled around in it in the dressing room, I imagined my Hurdy Gurdy Man, RobBob, and myself dancing the night away. We both loved to dance, but we only slow danced, so we slow danced to every song, pressing our bodies into each others. I was working weekends at Salet's this year and didn't have as much time to sew. I had made my dress last year for just five dollars without asking her for anything, so I felt that was in my favor too.

Oh, the formal dress was so cute. It was an A-line empire-style floor-length dress in pink taffeta, covered in pink lace with a pink felt ribbon and bow. I was sure Jackie Kennedy would have proudly worn it to some highbrow event.

Dad came thundering down the stairs and into the kitchen. He was stirred up and angry like a hornet. I could feel a fight was coming. It was a common event these days. I just kept my eyes on my job. He had his checkbook in his hand.

"What are all these checks made out to cash?" James loudly asked.

"It's my money too," answered Sandra.

"Well, we are overdrawn this month because of your nonspecific deductions. I want to know where that money is going," he demanded.

"Things just cost more these days, especially with a big family." She was cool as a cucumber.

"What big family? Jess and John are already out, and Jo works for her money." He threw the checkbook at her, causing her to spill her tea.

"Ouch!" she yelled, jumping up and now getting angry too. "Some men make enough money so their wives have nothing to worry about."

"And just who would that some man be? Dr. Androvich?" he yelled at her.

"Well," she hesitated. And then she yelled back, "Yes! Just like Dr. Androvich!"

"Just what I thought! Your Jackass Androvich!"

Sandra lunged at James, screaming, "Why, you stupid dunce! You don't know what you are talking about!" She pounded him with her fists.

"Like hell I don't. Why don't you tell me where Jimmy with the jet-black hair came from!" James pushed her away and slapped her hard on the back.

"Big man! I bet you feel better now." Sandra sneered, facing him again.

This time, James reached out, slapped her on the face, and said, "Yeah…now I do." He turned and walked out the door, slamming it shut.

Sandra ran to the door crying now and yelled out after him. "Big man! Go back to work, and get some more money to put in my checking account!"

"I'm not going to work today!" hollered James. "What do you think of that? Greedy lady!"

"We are not finished with this. Where are you going?" she screamed out.

"Fishing, 'cause if I stuck around here, I might kill you!" he yelled back.

I was standing by the sink. I turned around and saw Mother had gone back to her tea. I saw the slap mark on her cheek. It was a handprint.

Well, I thought. *Now she knows how that feels*. Then I had a smart thought. *I guess I won't ask for money. I will wear the same dress to prom that I wore last year. Robert loved it. He loved me in it. He loved it on the floor beside his bed.*

Chapter 25
The Blood-Red Fountain

"Go on, Jo. What did you do then?" asked Jacob, pulling me out of my meditation.

"I remembered it was Labor Day weekend. It is, isn't it? Labor Day weekend?" I asked.

"Yes. Is that meaningful?" he asked.

"Dad always goes fishing over Labor Day weekend. He hasn't told Mother where he goes in at least ten years. When I remembered that, I stood up with some relief. I picked up the bedroom telephone and called 911. How could he have done it if he was out of town? I gave them the address and told them what they would find.

"I can't tell you why I did not stay and wait for the police. I took Blackie in Robert's car back to my apartment in Owatonna and put him in the shower with me so we could both get cleaned up. I was overwhelmed with emotion, and I didn't know what to think or feel. In the shower, I watched the dirt from Blackie and the blood from us both go down the drain. We stayed in there, letting the water wash it all away until the water ran cold. In times like these, I long to feel close to God so I sang a hymn at the top of my lungs, as if to scare all the demons away."

I sat there and sang it for Jacob Sanders, audience of one. He did not interrupt me.

> There is a fountain filled with blood drawn from
> Emmanuel's veins; and sinners plunged beneath
> that flood lose all their guilty stains. Lose all their

guilty stains, lose all their guilty stains; and sinners plunged beneath that flood lose all their guilty stains.

The dying thief rejoiced to see that fountain in his day; and there may I, though vile as he, wash all my sins away. Wash all my sins away, wash all my sins away; and there may I, though vile as he, wash all my sins away.

Dear dying Lamb, thy precious blood shall never lose its power till all the ransomed church of God be saved, to sin no more. Be saved, to sin no more, be saved, to sin no more; till all the ransomed church of God be saved, to sin no more.

E'er since, by faith, I saw the stream thy flowing wounds supply, redeeming love has been my theme, and shall be till I die. And shall be till I die, and shall be till I die; redeeming love has been my theme, and shall be till I die.

Then in a nobler, sweeter song, I'll sing thy power to save, when this poor lisping, stammering tongue lies silent in the grave. Lies silent in the grave, lies silent in the grave; when this poor lisping, stammering tongue lies silent in the grave.[8]

Jacob sat there, silent. I don't know what he was thinking.
"Allesandra Lewis is silent in the grave," I said.
"Is that everything Jo?" Jacob seemed to believe me.
"I got dressed and went to work even though I was in a daze. I just didn't know what else to do. I was there until almost closing hours, before the police came and arrested me for the murder of my mother. What evidence do they have against me?"

---

[8] Text: William Cow, *The United Methodist Hymnal No. 622*, 1731–1800 (Public domain)

"Quite a bit, I'm afraid. Your fingerprints are the only ones on the knife—that is, the kitchen knife that you say you put there. They have your clothes from that morning with your mother's blood on them. They have your tennis shoe imprint in the blood. A hair that matches yours was found on her body. Your bloody fingerprints were on the phone in her bedroom. And then the most damning piece of evidence—your confession," said Jacob.

"Confession? What confession?" I hadn't remembered that yet.

Jacob shuffled a couple pieces of paper and found the one he wanted to read. "When they arrested you, you said you 'hated your mother.' You said you were 'glad she was dead.' You said you 'stabbed her with the kitchen knife' and that she got 'just what she deserved.' You said you 'sent the demon in red to hell where she belongs.'" Jacob sat back in the chair.

"I did?" I asked.

Jacob nodded yes, and he was frowning.

We sat there in silence for a few minutes while I pondered the evidence.

"That sounds about right," I finally said.

"Really?" Jacob was surprised.

"But I didn't do it," I said as I shook my head no.

"I guess I should tell you your sister will be testifying for the prosecution." Jacob was hesitant with this information.

"My sister?" I was baffled about that.

"Jessie was the one who identified your mother's body at the morgue. When she saw bruises on Allesandra's neck, she started screaming curses at you. She insists you killed your mother because you hated her. She says you tried to kill her too once by almost strangling her to death. She says she is terrified of you."

I sighed deeply. "Wow, well, I guess that is sort of true too. It was just a silly sibling fight." I had never found Jessie on my side ever before, so I wouldn't expect her to defend me now. "What happened to Dad's dog? I shut Blackie in my bedroom with a bowl of water. I hope someone found him and is taking care of him."

"He was taken to the dog pound," said Jacob.

"What day is it?" I asked.

"It is Tuesday, September 3," he responded.
"Dad will be back tonight," I said with confidence.
"You think?" he asked.
"I am pretty sure," I said.

Jacob got up to leave. Before the door shut, he said, "Everything's going to be okay Jo."

I can read faces. I don't think he meant what he said.

Once he left, I lay down on the cot and stared at the ceiling. I thought about the time Mother painted the kitchen ceiling.

Chapter 26
The Red Ceiling

When I was a small child, I did not think about whether my parents loved each other. I know I never felt love for or from my mother, but I assumed my dad loved her. I couldn't see how he would want to though because she was so mean. I never really questioned it until I got older. I heard them argue more and more as time went on, and Dad went off fishing more and more.

One summer day, on a Friday at the noon hour, I heard them go at it.

"James, let's go out for a cocktail and a steak dinner tonight at the Legion in Owatonna," Mother invited Dad. He was sitting at the dining room table, having just finished eating his lunch. She was standing by him with a hand on his shoulder. I was washing the lunch dishes while glancing at them in the next room.

"Not tonight, Sandra," said James.

"Why not?" questioned Sandra.

"When I get home, I want to relax," he answered her.

She began to rub his shoulders. "You never take me out anymore," she persisted.

"Don't say never. That is a gross exaggeration," he said.

"But I have a new dress that I want to show off," she said in a flirting way.

"What? Why would you buy a new dress when I told you money is tight," he said.

"Because I wanted it," she said, still teasing him.

RED

"We talked about this before!" James was raising his voice. "Money is tight with Johnny in college this year."

Sandra stopped rubbing his shoulders and backed away. "Why should I have to suffer so he can go to college? He should pay for it himself," she said.

"He will pay it back when he gets a job," he said.

"Some people have credit cards. I think I should have a credit card, and you can pay it off later when you get more money," said Sandra, sneering at him. "Or a better job," she added.

"I have never borrowed money, and I never will. I worked and slaved for you so you could have this big house. I work hard for the money, and you seem to have no common sense about it at all!" yelled James.

"Like I said, if you had a decent job, we wouldn't have to worry about the little things," said Sandra.

There was a pause.

"We do not have extra money for your frivolous wasting!" he yelled at her.

"Well, I work hard around here too, raising your kids, all of whom I never really wanted," she stabbed at him with her words. I felt a little stab myself.

"I sort of remember you wanting the one with the jet-black hair!" Dad shouted at her.

There was another pause.

"I have a vegetable garden to save money on the grocery bill, and I deserve to have fun and go out once in a while!" she yelled at him.

"Trouble is you want to go out all the time!" he yelled.

"Well, I have a new dress, and I want to wear it!" she yelled back.

"Well, you are not going to wear it. Let me guess. Is it red? Take it back! You can't afford it!" he shouted at her.

"You mean you can't afford it!" she screamed at him.

"Yes, you are right about that. I can't afford it. I can't afford you!" He got up and stormed out the door. Seconds later, he came back in, shouting, "Oh, and by the way, I hate the color red!" He slammed the door and took off.

Mother came in the kitchen, fixed herself a cup of tea, and sat at the kitchen table. She sipped her tea without ever putting the cup down. I could imagine her twisted mind was twirling. She was thinking deeply. "Hmmm," she said when she finally set the empty cup down and leaned back in her chair. She began tapping her fingers on the table. Suddenly, she got up and grabbed her purse. She opened it, found her lipstick, and refreshed her bright red lips.

"I am going to the hardware store, Jo. Make sure you finish cleaning up the kitchen," she said to me as she opened the door and walked out.

About a half an hour later, she returned, carrying her revenge—a can of bright red paint—and looking gleefully devilish.

I watched as she got a ladder from the garage, covered the kitchen floor with newspapers, and covered her hair with a rag from the rag drawer. Then she brought up a new painter's brush from the basement and began painting the kitchen ceiling, one stroke at a time, bright red, the exact color of her lips.

I checked on her periodically. "What are you doing?" I asked. "That paint really stinks."

"Just having some fun," she said. "Open a window for me, and leave me alone."

Mother finished with enough time to make supper and have it ready by six. I felt a little tense wondering how Dad would handle this situation because it looked like quite a situation to me.

He walked home from work and paused before the porch steps. By his demeanor, I could tell he was still in a bad mood. He spotted the used painter's brush in a glass jar of water on the top step. He picked it up, smelled it, and swirled the brush around a little. He carried it into the house with him. "Sandra!" he yelled.

"What?" she answered smiling. "You don't have to shout. I am standing right here."

"Were you painting something?" he asked.

"Why?" she asked. Her grin was getting bigger.

"Because I saw this new painter's brush with oil paint in it sitting in a jar of water. You have just ruined this brush. You have to clean up oil paint with turpentine," he explained.

"I don't like turpentine," she said. "It stinks."

"Well, you just wasted some more money today." He sounded very, very crabby. He set the jar down on the counter in the kitchen and walked into the dinning room and sat down at the table. Supper was ready.

Jimmy and I were already sitting there, waiting. We had been looking out the window for Dad to come home, watching to see what would happen next.

"You just don't care about money," crabbed James.

"Yes, I do." Sandra defended herself. "Actually, I like it very much."

"Well, what the hell did you paint?" James asked, sniffing the air.

Sandra couldn't hold in the joyous revenge any longer. She just burst out laughing. She had to sit down. She was laughing so hard.

"What did you paint?" James asked again. He couldn't be more annoyed with her.

"Dad," said Jimmy as he pointed up to the ceiling in the kitchen.

James turned his head up and looked. He gasped. He shoved his chair away from the table. He looked at Sandra who was crying now with her laughter.

James' face turned beet red with rage. It, too, was almost the color of the ceiling. Without saying another word, he left the house and slammed the door so hard the old glass window in it shattered. It was almost dawn before he returned from fishing.

Chapter 27
The Red Welts

Supper time blats from the loudspeaker warned me to get ready.

"Step away from the door," a piercing command came over the loudspeaker. I obeyed like a soldier. The door of my cell opened, and another command came.

"Step out and step into the line!" Women of all ages and color stepped into the same line. I still felt like a dumb sheep, but now I understood why I had been brought here.

I felt my mouth smile a fake smile, oh so fake, but my eyes, the windows to my soul, were still sad. Very sad.

I stepped in front of #11284774 and said, "Haven't I seen you somewhere before? Come on. Follow me to the Starlight Room for dinner and dancing."

She just shook her head and rolled her eyes. "What are you so happy about?" she whispered. "You are an assassin."

"And you are just an ass," I whispered back. I was feeling a little braver among the condemned.

She gave and extra hard shove and pushed me into #05135776 who turned around and shoved me back. Now they were just shoving me back and forth between the two of them like I was a blow-up free-standing punching bag with a cartoon face. That brought the matron running to the squirmish.

"No talking!" blared the loudspeaker.

Whack! Whack! Whack! We each got one square on our backs. She was efficient without saying a word. We three straightened up without saying a word. I shook off the pain. I had felt it before. It reminded me of a different *Whack! Whack! Whack!*

*****

It was date night in the Lewis house. I was fifteen. I had just made the cutest little blue pleated skirt that afternoon to wear with my new long-sleeved white sweater. It was just long enough that I knew I could get out of the house in it. Once outside, I planned to roll the waist band up a couple of times for the Twiggy effect. I put on nylons and slipped into black Mary Jane flats. I checked myself out in the mirror and hoped it would be eye-popping for Robert. I was so excited I just couldn't wait.

It would be my first time out on a real date with Robert where he was allowed to pick me up in his car. Of course, my curfew had to be ten o'clock. I had argued and argued with Mother for a later time all week. It was embarrassing to have to be home so early. What did it leave time for? A movie and an ice cream cone and then home again. I guess that was her intent.

While I was waiting for Robert, I tried again. "What are you thinking? Ten o'clock is no time at all," I begged.

"It is a proper time to be home from a date," stated Mother.

"Maybe proper time for a first-grader. I am a grown-up. I should be allowed to make my own choices," I pleaded.

"You can make your own choices when you move out," she was not budging.

"I don't remember Johnny ever having to be home so early?" I was bargaining.

"He's a boy!" Mother was raising her voice now.

"What difference does that make? I am sure he is dating a girl!" I yelled at her.

"Don't you dare raise your voice at me," she said through gritted teeth.

"I have to!" I screamed. "Otherwise, you never listen to me!"

"I hear you loud and clear, and if you keep this up, you won't go out at all," she said it slowly and distinctly, with an evil and hateful grimace on her face.

I could see she was just hoping I would bark some more at her, just one more time, so she could punish me. I know that demon in her feeds off punishing me.

I turned around and walked into the dining room where Johnny was sitting on a dining table chair. He was leaning back in it and rocking it with one arm on the table to push himself. He was laughing at me. "Go on, Jo. You are just stupid enough to give her another argument so you can stay home tonight." Then he threw his head back and just laughed again.

I couldn't turn my anger on Mother, and it definitely needed somewhere to go, so I put my foot up on the chair between his legs and pushed him over. He fell flat on his back and began cursing me. Now I was the one laughing. He got up as fast as he could and tore into me. We were wrestling and yelling, and I was definitely getting more and more upset because I knew I was getting my clothes and hair all messed up.

All of a sudden, I felt her rage against me. Three well placed whacks on the backs of my legs as hard as she could with a leather belt of Dad's. It put an immediate stop to the fight.

Shit, that hurt, I thought. I ran upstairs and took a look at the backs of my legs in the long bathroom mirror. The whipping had caused a run in the back of the left stocking, but worse than that, there were horrific red raised welts on the backs of both of my legs. My night was ruined.

I went to my room and shut the door. Of course, I was crying, but I wasn't going to make any noise with it. I leaned back against the door and sighed. Mascara was running down my cheeks.

How can I go out now with those marks on my legs? I thought. I saw Nadahunga on my bed. He always helped me think things through. I picked him up and held him tight until I heard Robert's car out front. Nudahunga must have given me the idea. I took off the nylons and put on white knee socks. They covered most of the cruel welts and matched my sweater.

Then I heard Mother giving Robert my curfew instructions and a lecture about proper behavior, on a date so I scurried down the stairs to save him. He didn't smile at me. He looked at me with surprise and then his frowning brow went up in the center of his forehead.

Why at a time like this when I needed his smile? I wondered.

"Are you ready?" he asked.

"Yes," I said meekly.

"You better go look in the mirror first," he said. He still wasn't smiling.

"Okay, wait a sec," I said and hurried to the downstairs bathroom to look in the mirror.

He was right. I was pretty pathetic-looking with mascara smeared under my eyes, and my hair was a mess. In my frustration and haste, I forgot to wash the mascara off my cheeks. No wonder I didn't get the smile.

I cleaned my cheeks and straightened my hair the best I could with my hands. Now I was a wounded soldier. I had no pride. I had no joy. I didn't really even want to go out any more. The joy of a first date had been deflated with a loud bang, like a needle stuck in a rubber party balloon.

As I walked through the kitchen and to the door, I paused and glanced into the dining room. She was calmly sipping tea at the dining room table. She looked up at me as that fake plastic smile crept across her face. "Have fun," she said.

My icy blue eyes spoke back to her. *I hate your living guts.*

I turned to the door without looking at Robert. We walked out to his car. He opened his door, and I slid in. We didn't talk on the drive to the movie. I was too embarrassed to tell him I got a whipping. He was too sensitive to ask me why I was forlorn.

The movie was *Viva Las Vegas*, starring Elvis Presley and Ann-Margret. It was a lighthearted musical comedy. I was feeling just the opposite—heavyhearted and morose. I didn't really watch it. I was thinking about my stinging legs and my wounded spirit. Robert reached his hand over to hold mine, and once our fingers entwined, I felt a little better. When the lights came up, we looked at each other. He gave me that green-eyed grin that I was longing for, and I smiled.

"Ice cream?" he asked.

"Sure," I said.

His affection for me was enough to still the woe inside.

*****

I followed the line down corridors of cells and into the cafeteria. I was more aware of all the prisoners for the first time.

"Poor girls, there must be other innocents here just like me. God help us all," I said to myself. I was not defeated by the stinging wound that I felt on my back. I had a positive feeling this would be my last meal with the inmates because I knew in my heart Dad was coming home tonight. He would make things right. But if he didn't do it, who did?

I refused to look directly at my tray until I sat down, all the while praying there would be something edible on it.

"Ohhhhh…" I sighed. One big nutraloaf. Somebody help me! All the leftovers from the week chopped up, stirred together, and pressed in to a loaf that was then fried in nasty grease on the grill.

That is not going to make it down my throat, I thought with huge disappointment.

But there was a cookie and a dozen grapes. I ate the grapes and the cookie as fast as I could so no food thief could get them. Then I chopped my loaf in half, pushing the halves apart and sat back and waited. I felt like I was setting bait for a couple of hungry wolves.

Just as I thought. A hand from my left and a hand from my right each reached over and grabbed a piece. This was what you call making friends.

CHAPTER 28
BEFORE I WAS BORN

The day was stiflingly hot. Allesandra Burnham sat on the trunk she had dragged out of the country house to rest in the shade of the lonely oak tree at the end of the dirt driveway. Her mother had given her the trunk.

"Take it. I don't want it," her mother, Edna, had whined, sounding more like an annoying sot than the English princess she claimed to be. The shiny black metal, the polished brass moldings, and the lock still looked as new as the day she got it twenty-four years earlier. The interior was lined with red Chinese silk. To Sandra, it smelled funny, but her mother insisted it was supposed to smell that way to keep the moths out.

Grandmother Morgan had purchased the trunk in England, filled it with as much as she could get into it, and migrated to America. Now everything Sandra owned didn't even begin to fill it. She didn't have much. Who did? These last few years were war years, and everyone had to sacrifice for the cause. However, now the war was over, and James was coming home. Sitting there, she could get a good look far down the road to watch for her ride. A little breeze moved her hair ever so slightly. It felt like hot breath from hell.

Please don't let me sweat, was her inner plea. *I've got to be fresh when James comes.*

Just to pass the time away, she thought of all the things she had packed in the trunk, like her neatly folded underwear. There was never enough underwear, so she had stolen a couple pairs from her sister, figuring she would be long gone before Cindy ever noticed.

Sandra chuckled, thinking of Cindy fussing about the lost underwear. She'd have to wash out the two pairs she had left, every other day. Sandra shook her head. No love lost there. But she didn't care. The only regard they ever had for each other was a good argument. Cindy was lazy. What did she ever do around there but play? She was skinny as a stick, with no breasts, and so immature. It was quite intolerable.

Her high school yearbook, filled with pictures of her friends, now closed to the making of new memories, lay in the bottom of the trunk so as not to crush anything. Sandra was one year out of high school, class of 1945. She had lightly hung on to one girl friend, Henrietta Bjornevik. They could be possibly stay friends, she thought.

In the trunk was her favorite red corduroy dress. Grandmother had made it. She loved that red dress. It fit her body like a glove, flaring out below her knees. That was the only flaw, so Sandra secretly shortened the hem by two inches. The shoulders were padded and decorated with military flap and brass buttons. The four-inch waistband came to a *V* at her navel. The long sleeves pushed up to her elbows. Very chic to say the least. Sandra couldn't remember having such a stylish dress before. Of course Papa wouldn't approve of her showing the knees even if they were barely peeking out from under, but what could he say now? Was it the dress, or was it just that she loved the color? It matched her spirit. Fiery red.

Then there was the hat to match. Clever Grandmother had actually made it out of cardboard and glue. It was a half a skull cap with a *V* shape pointing down the middle of her forehead, covered of course in red corduroy and decorated with red netting that came down over her eyes. A metal comb was sewed on the underside to hold it in place. Grandmother surprised Sandra with it after she copied the style from a hat she saw in the Sears and Roebuck catalogue. Sandra was thrilled when she saw it.

There were her red baby doll high-heeled shoes that her mother said only a whore would be brazen enough to wear.

"What does she know?" sneered Sandra. The shoes made her feel like dancing. She imagined herself out on the town in James' arms, dancing the night away. After all, that is how they met—at a dance hall in Owatonna. He was shy, but she had managed to get him out on the dance floor a few times. It was never enough to satisfy her high-spirited energy level.

There were the tiny red barrettes Papa had given her for Christmas. Papa was a big man, not so tall but quite rotund, weighing two hundred and fifty pounds. His oversized hands could easily reach completely around her biceps, an experience she knew only too well. That's where he grabbed her and gave a little shake if he felt she were not being proper enough. Papa had pampered her to the point of spoiling, but he was adamant she should act proper. Allesandra was his firstborn. He didn't even notice the other children who came after her. He was blind to the fact that this was the cause of severe sibling rivalry in his children, for they all longed to have his love and respect. They fought for equal favor, but there was none.

In the trunk were her nursing uniforms. She didn't think she would ever really wear them again. She was forced to leave nursing school early. Nursing school didn't allow married students. She didn't really care. She loved learning about all the diseases and felt she could already diagnose everything that was medically wrong with people. She had read all of her books completely, but she hated the sick people. They always were crabby with bad breath.

Edna had said she was a disgrace to the family for quitting school, a poor example to her younger siblings, but she just didn't care. James was coming for her. He would make everything right. The blasted war was over. His job on the aircraft carrier had never put him at the front lines of war, so his life had been spared unlike so many others. It seemed every family around there had beloved boys on the fatality list.

The one thing that should have been in the trunk but wasn't was the beautiful red and white double wedding ring quilt that Grandmother Morgan had made for her. Sandra had carefully chosen the colors for it. Every piece of fabric in it was brand new. Sandra was so sick of old things. Somehow, in some sneaky way, Edna, her mother put the quilt on her own bed. She insisted it was the only blanket that gave her the warmth she needed to get better. Because she was so sick all the time, Sandra just couldn't take it with her when she left. It wouldn't look proper.

They had been married just six weeks earlier. James was home from the navy for his thirty-day leave. Two days before deployment, Sandra coerced him into marriage. James wasn't sure he knew her well enough, but she sure was sexy and so easily aroused his passion.

Egads, he was gorgeous in that uniform, thought Sandra. He was the only beautiful part of her wedding. Sandra thought of that day with a little remorse. There was no white dress. There were no flowers. There was no music. There was no celebration party. There was the one important element however—love.

Love, sex, what's the difference, she thought. All she knew about him really was that he made her tingle all over when he touched her. It was a shotgun wedding, but she held the shotgun. The honeymoon only lasted two days before James was shipped out. She couldn't wait to be in his arms again. He would be her savior from this house of poverty.

God it was hot. Sandra wiped her sweaty hands on her freshly ironed dress and immediately cursed herself for it after seeing the oily marks they made.

She reached up her hand to shade her eyes from the broiling sun. She peered down the road.

"James! James!" Sandra said out loud. "Hurry up and get me. I've never been more ready for anything in all my life. Come and get me out of here!"

She loved saying his name. The thought of him sent shivers down her spine. Thinking about sex with him anyway did because that was about all she really did know about him. He was shy. She never really noticed him in high school, but when she saw him in his uniform at the dance hall, her favorite place to be, she determined he would be hers. He had something very important. He had a car.

She could remember every detail about him physically. Every strong feature in his handsome face was finely chiseled to perfection. His deep-set eyes were the color of purest chocolate. They sparkled with flames of amber when he was happy. She knew she made him happy because she gave herself to him after that very first night of dancing. His brown hair curled around in perfect waves that swooped down to touch his eyebrows. He was tan for he loved to be outside, usually fishing. He was taller than Sandra, but when she wore her red high heels, they were eye to eye, nose to nose, and cheek to cheek. His shoulders were broad and strong, with every muscle from there on down perfectly formed. Sandra thought his waist must be almost as small as hers, and those narrow hips led to the shapeliest legs she had ever seen on a man. Not that she had seen very many men's legs, but she knew what she liked.

The sound of a distant car brought her mind back from dreamland. Excitedly, she stood up and looked intently down the road. Yes, it was a car! Yes, it was a black. It was coming fast. Sandra could see the dust trail swirling up behind it. Yes, it was a Model A Ford. Yes! Yes! She could see him now behind the wheel. He still had his sailor uniform on. Yes, it was her beloved James.

Sandra couldn't help herself. She clapped her hands and jumped up and down with excitement. The car turned in the driveway and stopped. The door flew open, and as quick as lightning, they were locked in embrace. Without a word, they kissed until they were breathless.

"I love you, Sandra Lewis." She melted at the sound of his voice—a rich tenor voice that was truly music to her ears.

"I love you, James Lewis." They made love with their eyes, their vision locked intently on each other. They both felt totally complete as nothing had ever made them feel before.

"I love you, Sandra Lewis," he said it again for they were the only words that came to his mind. Sandra was a beautiful woman, and she wanted him. She took his hand, and they slowly walked up to the house to say goodbye to her childhood.

When they stepped inside the kitchen, feelings that Sandra didn't expect crept into her heart. Grandmother and her sister, Cindy Lou, were sitting at the kitchen table, cutting quilt blocks. Sandra reached down to hug Grandmother from behind and breathed in the familiar rose water scent.

"Only a brazen hussy would wear perfume," her mother had said. Sandra was sure Grandmother was no hussy.

"I think you are the only one I am going to miss, Gran," Sandra whispered in her ear.

"Allesandra, dear, I shall pray every day that the good Lord keeps you safe from harm's way," said Grandmother.

Sandra wondered what made grandmother have a close relationship with God. Sure, Sandra believed in God. It was the proper thing to do, but she didn't think God cared about her problems. She was sure he had bigger things to worry about. Yet if she wasn't proper in all aspects of her life, she sure wasn't going to let anyone else know about it.

Yes, Sandra was proper—too proper to tell anyone the real reason she left school. She told Papa and Mother she just hated nursing and couldn't go through with it to graduation. She told Henrietta, her best friend, she was so in love with James that she just couldn't wait another year.

"You have only known him a month," said Henrietta. "A year would be nothing."

"What would you know anyway?" asked Sandra. "I don't think you have ever even been on a date."

Henrietta was not offended. She really wasn't that interested in dating yet, and she admired Sandra for her straightforward personality.

She told the school authorities her mother was very sick and needed her at home full-time. She told James it was because she had told Papa they had had intimate relations, and if they didn't get married right away, Papa would blow his blasted head off. She was pretty good at manipulating everyone around her, and she was not afraid to lie.

"Take everything to the Lord in prayer, Allesandra," said Grandmother.

"I will," Sandra said it truthfully, even though she wasn't sure if there was a God. Pray? Yes, Sandra prayed. In fact, every day for two months now, she prayed earnestly. "Dear, God, please kill this baby inside me so no one will know I wasn't proper."

She glanced at Cindy. *No way. Those can't be tears on her cheeks,* Sandra thought to herself. *She hates me.*

"Cindy," she said out loud. Cindy looked up and burst out sobbing. Sandra just laughed out loud. That sent Cindy running up the stairs. Grandmother gave Sandra an annoyed look.

"What?" said Sandra. "What did I do? She is just mad that I am leaving because now she will have to do my job around here."

She shrugged her shoulders and walked into the sitting room. Shirley, another sister, was curled up on the horse hair fainting couch, reading a book. How anyone could sit comfortably on horse hair was beyond her comprehension. It pricked and scratched, even through clothes.

Who ever designed that idea? Even more curious, who would buy it? wondered Sandra. And there would be no replacing it, for it just never wore out. Shirley was a loner. Looking at her now, Sandra realized she didn't know much about her. She always had her nose in a book.

"Well, too late now," she said to herself. "Because I am out of here."

Libby, another sister, was playing the pump organ, accompanying her own off-key laments. *Why doesn't someone tell that poor pathetic thing she can't sing?* Sandra wondered.

"I guess it's goodbye," said Sandra.

Libby stopped playing, swung around, and stood up.

"Bye. I'll write and tell you everything you are missing out on around here," she said.

"I won't hold my breath waiting for a letter," answered Sandra, not really caring. "I'm not going that far away, stupid." She thought Libby was simple, naïve, and easy to take advantage of. Sandra had taken advantage of her plenty of times. Libby had become her little gopher, as in "go get this" and "go get that" and "go do this" and "go do that." She loved ordering her around.

"Don't let the door hit you in the butt," Shirley snickered.

"My, what an unpleasant child," said Sandra. Her sisters were younger. Ever since she could remember, she thought of herself as an adult, and in her mind, her siblings merely stayed little children. How was that possible?

Back in the kitchen, James sat with Grandmother. He was simply nodding politely. That's all the encouragement Gran needed to ramble on and on. She smiled, knowing how shy James was.

"Allesandra," her mother, Edna, called in the most pathetic voice she could muster.

Slowly and not wanting to go in, Sandra walked into the bedroom off the other side of the kitchen. Edna lay in the center of the big white-painted iron bed. It was a work of art, with the spindles and molded rosebuds. It was the only piece of furniture in the whole house Sandra thought was worth anything at all.

Edna was covered with a brand-new red and white double wedding ring quilt. It was pulled up to her chin, and Edna was gripping the top edge of it on either side of her face with her feeble white hands. This was Sandra's quilt. Grandmother had made it for her recent marriage, but somehow, the ailing English princess had weaseled it onto her bed and there it stayed.

For now, thought Sandra. *But I will get that quilt sooner or later.* The bed and the blanket were beautiful. Mother was not. Her long gray hair was thin but neatly braided and wrapped around the top in a unique way. Unique because Sandra fixed it different every time, never quite knowing just what to do with it. Sandra wouldn't miss fixing it. She hated touching it unless it was freshly washed, and that wasn't very often.

Maybe now she'll get it bobbed and styled, thought Sandra. *After all, she can't reach her poor little arms up there to fix it herself. And none of those pathetic sisters of mine will be able to help her."*

Mother was almost always in this bed with some kind of infirmity. The headache, the neckache, the back ache, the stomach ache, the leg ache. In fact, if you could name it, it ached.

"There you are, Allesandra, dear. I don't know what I shall ever do without you." Mother's voice was filled with melodramatic self-pity.

Sandra certainly knew what she was going to do without her psychosomatic mother. She spelled *Freedom* with a capitol *F*. With just one of the required three years of nursing school behind her, Sandra had diagnosed Edna as psychosomatic. No doctor ever found a thing wrong with her even though she had hundreds of complaints, and Sandra, the eldest, was expected to wait on her hand and foot.

She would not miss the ever constant call. "Allesandra! Shut my door. Allesandra! Keep the kids quiet. Make me something to eat. Bring me a book. Call the doctor. Get my medicine. Fix my neck. Fix my pillow. Fix my leg. Fix it, fix it, fix it."

You don't just have pain, Mother. You are a pain, thought Sandra to herself. Out loud, and because she was proper, she said, "Goodbye, Mother dear. I shall miss you."

"Not," she said to herself.

"Take care of the trunk," whined Mother. "It doesn't have a scratch on it. The trunk is special. It will bring you good luck, dear."

"Yes, Mother," answered Sandra.

Why would I care about a trunk? she thought. *Just a hideous antique.* She was destined for a new life and new things.

Grandmother said there was no such thing as luck. Good things that happened were blessings from God. Sandra wasn't sure about either one.

"Kiss me goodbye then, dear," squeaked Edna. Sandra bent down and touched her mother on the forehead with two fingers. She cringed at the thought of placing her lips on her mother's skin.

"Goodbye, Mother," she tried to say it with kindness for that would be the proper thing to do, but it sounded cold—very cold.

Relief flooded her spirit as she left the bedroom. Nineteen years of catering to that whining woman had come to an end.

Sandra surveyed Mother's kitchen. She looked down at the unpainted wooden floor that creaked in a hundred places.

It will probably never be this clean again now that I am leaving, she thought.

In the center of the room was the oak pedestal table that had to have enough leaves to accommodate as many guests as they had ever had. There was a slop bucket under the sink that all too often stunk. How the pigs ever gobbled that stuff up was beyond her comprehension. The pump on the sink that Grandmother had stencil painted was worn-looking from constant use. The only thing she thought she might miss was the tasty well water, knowing how awful city water was with chlorine in it.

They were beginning to modernize, although it didn't seem important to Papa. They did have a fancy electric refrigerator and a telephone but no indoor plumbing, which meant no proper bathroom. Papa said the day hell froze over would be the day he'd put in an indoor crapper.

"Good bye poverty, and good riddance to this dump," Sandra said to herself.

"I'm ready, James. Let's go outside and find the boys." She turned to walk out. James leapt up and grabbed Sandra's hand, glad to be on his way.

Outside in the shade of the overhang stood Papa in his denim overalls, smoking a cigarette. Sandra looked at him with distaste.

Denim. Ugh, she thought. *I will never wear denim again. It is the fabric of a poor dirt farmer—the covering of poverty.* Denim overalls were practically a uniform that never wore out. Each pair was just handed down to the next child who happened to be growing into that size.

Her brothers, Ike and Jake, were wrestling in the yard. When the boys saw Sandra, they stopped and ran over to bid her farewell. They were younger than all the sisters. They were about the same size, with the same straight dirty blond hair that was totally unmanageable. Both were skinny as rails, had bright blue eyes, very deep dimples, and very big hands. Those hands were a dead give away that Papa was their father. When they reached out to hug Sandra, she stiff-armed them.

"No, don't touch me!" she shrieked. "You're dripping wet and filthy." This rejection was normal, so they took off around the corner of the house and disappeared. "Goodbye, boys!" Sandra called after them, regaining her proper composure. "It's so hot. How can they stand to play like that? Did you see they were dripping wet with sweat? They are always so dirty."

Sandra hated dirt. She hated sweat, and she pretty much hated the boys. They were just a lot of extra work. How could any woman in her right mind have more babies if she was so sick all the time? But then her mother wasn't just any woman. She was an English princess.

Ha! If that's true, pondered Sandra. *Why are we so poor?*

Papa stepped forward smiling. There were a million things he wanted to say to this beautiful daughter of his. They flooded his mind but the words wouldn't form at his mouth.

From the day she was born, she was everything he had ever wanted his wife to be. She was vibrant. She loved life. She was healthy; so unlike Edna. He loved her shoulder-length brown hair; so thick you could hardly get a brush through it. He knew because he had brushed it many times when she was little. She was intelligent. He was so proud of her straight *A* grades in school. She was hard-working. She always took up the slack around the home front when Edna was bedridden with some vague infirmity. And she was feisty. Oh, how he loved that strong-willed nature. When her feathers were ruffled, it just made him laugh to see that feisty spirit snap to attention. He encouraged it.

"You're the love of my life," he wanted to say, sick as that was, but instead, he said, "You're a lucky man, James."

"Good bye, Papa. I'm not going to the end of the world, just a few miles away," said Sandra.

Papa Burnham hugged his firstborn grown-up daughter. She did not hug back. She was cringing at the thought of the dirt he would be leaving on her dress. His eyes filled with tears, and his throat was choked with emotion.

Good grief, thought Sandra as she pushed away from Papa's embrace. It always made her uncomfortable. *I won't have to tolerate that anymore,* she thought. Inside, she was recoiling, but on the surface, she held her head high in that ever so fake smile.

"Come on James, I'll help you put the trunk in your car," offered Papa. James looked at Sandra for approval. She nodded.

When she finally hopped in the car, James sighed a sigh of relief. She could tell he was uncomfortable. Maybe he was thinking of the threatening lie Sandra had told him about getting his head blown off. She chuckled at the thought of that. She was not sorry for the lie.

Sandra knew Papa's life would be more difficult without her, but that was his problem now. She wanted to yell at him to go get a job in town and quit trying to eek out a living on this godforsaken dirt farm. They were descendants of a queen of England, even if it was on Mother's side. They were not supposed to be paupers.

She really believed she was the only one who ever did anything productive around the farm. Whose name would Mother be calling from the bedroom now? Oh well, as long as it wasn't hers. She felt wonderfully free.

Mr. and Mrs. James Lewis drove away slowly. Neither were in a hurry anymore. Sandra sat as close to James as she could get, with her hand on his leg and an arm around his neck. It was hot and sticky, but James wasn't about to complain. Anyone who noticed the car might have thought it was driven by Siamese twins. He felt complete with her little body pressed against his. Hot, yes, but complete.

CHAPTER 29
THE RED CORDUROY DRESS

The newlyweds had no money. Sandra had an unrealistic dream that they could live on love. They could not afford a place of their own, so they moved in with James's mother, Clara Lewis, in Havana. James promised it would be for only a short while.

Clara removed all her personal things from the upstairs of her home. She preferred the downstairs bedroom anyway. That way, James and Sandra could have the whole upstairs "to themselves," she had said. There were two small bedrooms with a bathroom on one side of the upstairs and a third bedroom with a nursery on the other. James took the smallest bedroom for his office.

Initially, Sandra thought everything would be wonderful, but it was only days before Clara got on her nerves. She left Sandra alone unless James was around. When James was not working, Clara was always trying to be between them. It got old real quick. Clara obviously did not know the meaning of "to themselves."

Sandra did her best to try to get James out of the house once in a while. She pleaded with him to take her out dancing. She was eager to wear her red corduroy dress before it was too small in the waistline. Every attempt failed. James had lots of good excuses. Sandra was bored for lack of anything to do.

"I'm too tired. I'm too busy. I'm too tired. Too many other things are more important. I'm too tired," were his excuses. After all he was working hard and saving money to buy a house of his own. Sandra was impatient with this setup and was wishing she were still in school, or anything, to get out of the house and away from Clara.

She surveyed Clara's small library of boring books and read every one of them in the first month.

Sandra was already four months pregnant before she told James about it. For some reason, she felt she had to keep the lie going and told him she was three months along.

When James later told Clara Sandra was pregnant, Clara had a fit so ferocious it sent her to her bed for three days. It was bad enough she had to share James with this hussy. Now there would be an infant who would take away more of his attention from her.

After a couple of months, Sandra knew she had to find a doctor to care for her condition. She opened the phone book, and the first doctor in the list was a Dr. Jackson Androvich.

What the heck, she thought. *I'm sure he is as good as any.*

She called and made an appointment.

When the appointed time came, Sandra rummaged through her clothes to find something to wear to the doctor. Nothing seemed quite right. Finally, she pulled out the red corduroy dress. She mulled over the pros and cons.

"It's a bit flashy. It's bright. I feel good in it. James won't take me dancing in it. Clara won't let me go to church in it. Yes," she said. "I will wear it to the doctor."

With a decision made, she put on her red dress, rolled a pair of nylons up her sexy legs, and slipped her feet into the bright red baby doll high-heeled shoes. Next, she used a little black mascara to perk up her eyelashes, and she put on her gold wire glasses. The necessary spectacles did not deter from her beauty. Now she could see better to expertly paint her lips bright red. There was a full-length mirror behind the door of the bedroom. Sandra looked at herself in it for a few minutes, turning from side to side and patting her abdomen. It was tight, but she could manage it. She pushed the waistline up just a bit, causing it to be only a tad shorter at the hemline.

Now heading down the stairs, she called out to James in his office.

"James, I am taking the car to Owatonna for my doctor appointment."

"Okay!" he yelled back, not bothering look up from his desk."

*****

"Mrs. Lewis?" a nurse called into the waiting room of the medical clinic. Sandra stood up. "Please follow me," the nurse said with a big smile.

Sandra was ushered into Dr. Androvich's examining room. She had never been sick, and this was her first baby, so she was not sure what to expect.

After a boring fifteen-minute wait, Dr. Androvich knocked on the door, opened it, and stepped in, closing it with his foot as he was studying her brief written information. Looking up at her, he put out his hand and said, "Hello, Mrs. Lewis. I am Dr. Androvich."

Sandra stood up, took his hand, and said, "Hello."

He didn't let go. Sandra didn't know what to do, wondering what would be proper. She gave her hand a little tug back, but he still gripped it tightly. It seemed a minute went by, and he was staring at her without saying a word. She couldn't read his face.

Well, this is uncomfortable, thought Sandra. She finally and firmly pulled her hand back and sat down.

Dr. Androvich sighed and sat down too. "What can I do for you today, Mrs. Lewis. Allesandra, is it?" he asked.

"Yes," said Sandra. "I am quite sure I am pregnant."

"When was your last period?" Dr. Androvich spoke directly.

Sandra squirmed a little in her chair. She was not comfortable discussing personal things with strange men. "About five months ago," she ventured without looking directly at him.

"All right then, let's have a look," he said. "Take everything off and put that gown on. Sit up on the table, and I will be back in a few minutes." Out he went.

She struggled to unzip the dress. *Oh, brother*, thought Sandra. *I will wear something pullover next time.*

She removed all her clothes except her underpants, put on the hospital gown, and tied it securely shut. A nurse peeked in to check on her. "Naked under there?" asked the smiling nurse.

"Except for my underpants," said Sandra.

"Sorry," said the nurse. "Those must come off too. Dr. Androvich will be in in a minute."

Sandra could feel herself blush as she slipped off her panties and climbed back up on the table. She was feeling dread as she suspected what might come next. After all, she was practically a nurse herself. She had just never been a patient.

Dr. Androvich knocked and opened the door again. "All ready for me?" he said as he raised his eyebrows in a little flirt.

Sandra was stunned. She recognized a flirt. She refused to respond to it. He checked her blood pressure; looked in her ears, eyes, and throat; listened to hear heart and her breathing, stood back, and smiled at her. "Everything so far looks very healthy," he said. "Now put your feet in the stirrups, and lie back down please." Dr. Androvich was grinning. "We will check you out and see just how far along you are." He sat on his little rolling stool and scooted himself to the foot of the table.

Sandra didn't move. She thought she just might have to get up and get dressed and go home. Dr. Androvich snapped on a pair of rubber gloves.

Just then, the nurse came in and relieved Sandra's emotional pressure.

"Come on, Mrs. Lewis, swing your legs over there, and put your feet in the stirrups." She was reassuring. She held Sandra's hand and patted it. Sandra submitted to the powers that be. She closed her eyes and told herself she would never get pregnant again.

"There we are," said Dr. Androvich as he pulled off his gloves and threw them in the trash can. He stood up. "You can sit up now."

Gladly, Sandra sat up. "Well?" she asked impatiently.

"If you are looking for confirmation, yes, you are definitely pregnant. But I surmise you are fully aware of that. Everything looks good, and I believe you to be about five months along already. You have been hiding it well." Dr. Androvich grinned at her. Sandra didn't respond. "Do you have any questions for me?" he asked.

"Any chance of the baby being overdue?" Sandra asked.

"Hmmm." Dr. Androvich had never been asked that before. "Well, possibly a week or so."

"Hmmm," responded Sandra.

"Well, I will look forward to seeing you in six weeks." Again with the flirty eyebrows and grin. Sandra did not know what to make of that. "Make your next appointment on your way out. You can get dressed now. Bye." He went out, and the nurse followed him.

Sandra sighed deeply. She got dressed, made her next appointment, and went home.

*****

When James heard the car pulling in the driveway, he bounded down the stairs and met Sandra at the door. He watched her get out of the car and was flabbergasted at her outfit.

"Hey, where were you?" he asked. Maybe he misunderstood where it was she went.

"I went to see a doctor because I am with child. Did you forget?" It irritated her that he didn't give her all his attention as she expected he should.

"You dress up like that to see a doctor?" he asked. He held the door for her as she came inside the house.

"Dr. Androvich didn't seem to mind," she said, teasing.

"All right," he relented his disagreement. She sure was beautiful, and he sure loved her.

"How did it go, Sandra?" he asked.

"I am four months along, just as I suspected," she lied. "And all is well."

"Dancing, did you say you want dancing?" He pulled her in close and danced around the kitchen with her.

Clara walked in to start supper and was disgusted with them. She showed her disapproval in her face, in her posture, and in her rude comment.

"Hussy!" she said, and she walked back out.

"Why you ——!" Sandra called after her with gritted teeth, and James could have sworn she growled. He held her tight, or she would have followed Clara into the living room to argue some more. She was a feisty one.

"Come on, ignore her. We can't let this breathtaking outfit go to waste. Let's go up to the American Legion on Broadway in Owatonna. We'll get something to eat. I'll have a drink, and you can have some milk for the baby. We will dance 'til your feet hurt."

"Really?" Sandra was excited in her disbelief.

"Really," said James. And they did.

Unfortunately for Sandra, that was the very last night James ever took her dancing.

*****

The next four months were barely tolerable for Sandra. James worked and ate his mother's food and slept and catered to his mother. He felt he owed her because he paid no rent. After all, she was making it possible for him to save more money to buy his own house in the future—a prize he kept his eyes on.

Sandra felt disregarded, but because she wanted to be proper, she gradually gave up hounding James for his attention. She was already disenchanted with her short marriage. While she jealously watched him cater to his mother, she found solace in reading books. She began making a trip to the Owatonna library part of her weekly routine. It became an obsession, for when she was mentally living in the book that she was reading, nothing else around her mattered for those hours. At least James let her take the car pretty much whenever she wanted it.

*****

James rushed Sandra to the hospital with great excitement when Sandra was in labor. He didn't expect the baby for another month, so he was very concerned. To everyone's surprise except Dr. Androvich's and Sandra's, the first baby was premature.

CHAPTER 30
THE RED LAKE

Tuesday, September 3, Afternoon

James had just driven the six-hour trip home from Red Lake where he loved to go fishing every chance he had. Labor Day weekend was a father and son tradition. It was a rustic experience with no plumbing, no electricity, and no communication from the outside world. He loved the lonely quiet on the northern edge of the lake. It was still wilderness there. John was already off to college, so it was just James and Jimmy this year. Jimmy didn't talk much, and James appreciated it. This year, James needed the quiet to think.

They had fished most of every day. They ate as much fish as they could—fish for breakfast, fish for lunch, and fish for supper—and what they weren't going to eat, they set free back into the water. The weather had cooperated, and James felt rested, but he was far from relaxed. The first few years that he was married he thought he would never want to leave Sandra overnight, but as the years crept by, she grew colder, more distant, and always encouraged him to go and stay as long as he wanted.

James pulled into Havana about dusk on the day after Labor Day. As he pulled into the driveway, panic seized him. There was yellow and black police tape—the type of barrier used to isolate, protect, and preserve a crime scene—all around his house. When he stepped out of his car, an officer parked in the street called out to him on the bullhorn.

"This is a restricted area!"

James's heart began to race. "But I live here."

"Mr. James Lewis?" an officer called out as he got out of his car and walked toward James.

"Yes!" James shouted back.

"Who is that with you?" questioned the officer.

"My son, Jimmy," answered James. "This is my house. What is going on?"

"Where have you been?" asked the officer.

"We just got back from fishing in Red Lake. What has happened here? Where is my wife?" James asked.

"You and your son will have to come with me to the police station for questioning," replied the officer.

"Why? What is going on? Please tell me. Where is my wife, Allesandra?" James pleaded.

"Please get into the back of my car, and I will take you there. A court recorder will want to get your statement." The officer was calm and professional, wanting to keep the situation in control.

"My statement? I don't have a statement. I don't know anything. Help me please. Tell me what happened to Sandra? Is she alright?" James sounded anxious.

"I am sorry to tell you, sir. Your wife is at the Steel County Hospital. She is dead, sir. She is in the morgue." The officer was matter-of-fact.

"What! You must be joking! How did this happen?" James looked like he was really shocked.

"Sir, that is all I can tell you for now. You will receive complete information at the police station. Now please get in," insisted the officer.

James climbed into the back of the police car. Jimmy followed him in, but before he got in, he turned to the officer and said, "Ein dah one dat gotted buuned."

CHAPTER 31
DISAPPOINTMENT

Tuesday, September 3, Late Evening

"Lights out!"

I heard the blaring of the loudspeaker. By now, I knew it meant eleven o'clock at night. My heart sank. I had expected Dad, but he had not come for me. My deepest fears were met with profound agony with the possibility that my dad really did kill my mother, and I was in jail for what he had done in an explosive fit of rage. I lay down on my cot but was unable to even close my eyes, let alone fall asleep. I began to think more clearly now because my memory was feeling healthier. The shock had worn off, and now I realized I had to figure things out or I would never get out of here. I stared into the dark while I tried to put the facts together.

*****

James and Jimmy were ushered into the police station for questioning, where they were put in separate rooms. James sat in silence, pondering the situation, while Jimmy was questioned first. James was getting nervous, as it seemed an hour must have passed.

A social worker entered the room and sat down across from him.

"Hello, Mr. Lewis," she said. "My name is Renee Sorenson. I am from social services. First, let me say how sorry I am about the loss of your wife. This must be just a terrible shock to you and a terrible feeling of loss."

James just nodded and sighed.

"I have just spent some time with your son, Jimmy. He is very sweet." She smiled.

"You can say it," said James. "It is no secret that he is simpleminded."

"I, of course, have noted his obvious mental handicap and was wondering if there was someone I could call to come and get him and possibly keep him overnight. You will be here for a much longer time, and I don't see any reason for him to just sit here and wait." She had a pen and pad of paper in hand, prepared to write the information.

"Ah, yes, a neighbor of mine, Mrs. Henrietta Bjornevik. Her phone number is 448-3510. She lives across the street from me at 45 Second Street SW. I am sure she would be the most likely person to take him," said James. "He is very comfortable with her as well."

"All right then, Mr. Lewis. I will see he has supervision, at least for the next twenty-four hours, so you won't need to worry about him. You will not be able to go back into your house, as it is still a crime scene. Where will you be staying?"

"I guess I could go to my daughter Jo's apartment in Owatonna. I am sure she will let me sleep on her couch for as long as necessary," said James.

"Oh…O…kay," said Renee, just realizing he had not yet been informed of his daughter's arrest. "Well then," Renee got up and went to the door. "Good evening to you. sir." She went out to take care of Jimmy.

A detective entered the room and sat down across from James. "Hello, James," he said. "My name is Detective Anderson. I have many questions for you, and I am sure you will have some for me as well."

James nodded his head and looked down.

"First and foremost you already know your wife was found murdered early Saturday morning," stated Detective Anderson.

James looked up. "Murdered?" questioned James. "The officer said dead. He never said murdered."

"Where were you Saturday morning?" the detective asked.

"I was up at Red Lake," said James.

"Why?" asked the detective?

"I took Jimmy up there Friday night for our annual Labor Day fishing trip. We have gone fishing every Labor Day weekend for many years now," said James.

"And you just arrived home from there late this afternoon?" asked the detective.

"That is correct," said James.

"So from late Friday night until sometime this morning, you were at Red Lake."

"Yes."

"All right, here is a pen and pad of paper. It would be helpful if you could write down a timeline of your entire trip and any persons in any places who could corroborate your story."

James took the pen.

"I will let you do that after we are finished here," said detective Anderson. "What was your wife doing at the time you left town?" he asked.

"Ah, she was upstairs. I suspect she was going to read something. I hollered up goodbye. She said goodbye, and I left," answered James. He was feeling the torture of the night all over again and put his face in his hands.

The detective wrote down everything James said.

"Who found Sandra?" James asked.

"There was an anonymous 911 call to the police station around seven in the morning on Saturday. The police went to your home immediately and found Sandra expired. After assessing the crime scene, your daughter Jo was arrested for murder around six in the evening, Saturday."

James jumped up. "My daughter Jo! No way! Jo would never do anything like that. You have made a huge mistake." He punched the table with his fist. "Jo, where is Jo?"

"Please sit down Mr. Lewis. I know this situation is a great shock to you in many ways." Detective Anderson had an authoritative way. He had done this a few times before.

"No. You don't understand." He pounded the table with both fists. "Jo is innocent. I am sure of it. Where is she?"

"Please calm down, Mr. Lewis, and you will get all the necessary facts," said the detective.

James sat down.

"She is in the Steele County Detention Center," the detective informed him.

"Why? Why was she arrested? She couldn't possibly have done it," insisted James.

"Well, there is quite a bit of evidence that I cannot disclose to you at this time, but she did confess to the murder as well," said the detective.

James put his head in his hands again and rested his elbows on the table. "Oh my god! This can't be happening. Do you have any other suspects?"

"No. Do you know of anyone who would want to cause harm to your wife?" asked the detective.

"An intruder, a robber?" ventured James.

"There is no evidence of a robbery. It looks very much like a domestic," said the detective. "Can you think of anyone else at all who, for any reason, might want to cause harm to your wife?" asked the detective.

"Nnnno... Maybe...ah...yes, maybe." James was desperately thinking.

"Would you like to tell me?" pressed the detective.

"He...um... She..." he sighed deeply. "I believe Sandra may have been having an affair with Dr. Jackson Androvich."

"Do you know him?" asked the detective.

"No, not really," responded James. "Not in a personal way, but he has been our family physician ever since we were first married."

"How long have you suspected this?" asked the detective.

"I never did like him. Sandra was always crazy about him. I admit I have always had strange feelings about him. Sandra is so sexy. She is very beautiful." He stopped and broke down crying.

Detective Anderson pushed a box of tissue within his reach and waited for James to get control of himself.

"*Was* very beautiful," James continued. "But I didn't really think either of them would dare cross the line completely. We have four children, you know? I don't really know anything for sure."

"Okay, Mr. Lewis. Please complete that timetable for me, and I will have an officer take you to your house to get your car. Is there somewhere else you can stay until the crime scene has been released?" he asked.

"Yes, I can stay at my mother's house just a few blocks from there," said James.

"Okay. Include that address in your statement," said the detective.

"What about Jo? When can I see Jo?" he questioned.

"Well, right now, I am not sure. At present, she is under psychiatric care and evaluation and also suicide watch," said detective Anderson. "I will let you know when she is allowed visitors."

"Suicide watch? Oh no, my little Jo, no." James shook his head back and forth as he pushed away from the table and stood up.

"Will you be okay, Mr. Lewis?" asked the detective. He opened the door to leave.

James only nodded and deeply sighed. He sat back down, took the pen, and wrote down his deposition.

CHAPTER 32
DR. ANDROVICH

Detective Anderson went to Owatonna Hospital first thing in the morning. He found his way to the office of Dr. Androvich where a receptionist ushered him in to see the doctor.

"Good morning, Dr. Androvich. My name is Detective Anderson." He showed his badge. "I need to ask you a few questions about Mrs. Allesandra Lewis, a former patient of yours."

Dr. Androvich was sitting at his desk. He did not flinch at the sound of her name. He did not stand but gestured toward an empty chair in front of the desk.

"Yes, she is a patient of mine," he said. "Please sit down. What can I help you with?"

"Could you tell me what your relationship is with her?"

"I am her doctor…err…*was* her doctor."

"So you know then she was murdered."

"I have seen the news. I was very sorry to hear it. She was a lovely woman. Actually, I thought the entire family was very nice. I am acquainted professionally with all of them." Dr. Androvich sat back in his chair with a confident smile. "I delivered all four of her children."

"Have you ever seen Mrs. Lewis outside of the necessary professional visits?" began Detective Anderson.

"No," said Dr. Androvich. "Why would you ask me that?"

"I have reason to believe there was a personal relationship between the two of you," continued the detective.

"No." He was adamant. He frowned and shook his head from side to side.

"Well, you can tell me all of the truth right now, or you can come down to the police station with me for further interrogation," said the detective.

"Why?" asked the doctor. "How could I be a suspect? I heard her daughter was already arrested for the murder."

"That is true, but the case is far from closed. And Jo has not been arraigned yet due to her emotional difficulties. Were you having an affair with Allesandra Lewis?" asked the detective.

"No," said Dr. Androvich, but he was smiling now.

"What would you say if I told you I have a witness who put your car in the street near her house Friday night, August 30, the very night she was murdered," said the detective.

He's lying for sure, he thought. "A witness? What witness?" asked the doctor.

"She is a close friend of Mrs. Lewis's who lives across the street," said the detective.

Dr. Androvich burst out laughing, then slapped his left palm to his forehead. "Oh brother. All right, detective. You got me. Yes, we were having an affair, but I am a married man and so is…err… was she. We were just having some fun. We always had fun. It was just sex—a little cat and mouse game that went on for years. We weren't hurting anyone else, and I would have never killed her. I loved her."

Detective Anderson was appalled that Dr. Androvich could be so sociopathic about this situation. How could he laugh when a woman has been murdered, especially a woman he says he loves? "Were you with her in her home last Friday night?" he asked.

"No," said Dr. Androvich. He folded his arms across his chest.

"We have evidence from the crime scene, and there are a few jet-black hairs that, from what I can see, match your hair, so I am asking you to provide me with a sample of your hair," said Detective Anderson.

"Sure, sure, I'll give you that," said Dr. Androvich laughingly.

"You can stop in at the police station at your convenience within the next twenty-four hours," ordered the detective. "Now I have to ask you again. Were you with her in her home last Friday evening?" he asked.

"Yes," said the doctor. He covered his face with his hands and rubbed his forehead with his fingers to cover the guilty smile that was on his face.

"Did you have sex with her there?" asked detective Anderson.

"Yes," said the doctor. It was plain he decided to give up the truth.

"Did you get in a fight with her?"

"No," said Dr. Androvich.

"Did you kill her?" Detective Anderson was straightforward.

"No." He looked up at the detective. He laughed again. "We were just having some fun."

"What time did you leave?" questioned the detective.

"Well, I know I was home by midnight that night, so I suppose I left around eleven thirty. But I did not kill her. She was alive and well, very well, when I left," admitted the doctor. He wanted to, but he just couldn't get the smirk off his face. It was the face of insolence, like a boy who got caught playing a joke on his teacher.

"Weren't you nervous that her husband might come home and find the two of you together?" asked the detective.

"Heck no. He was off fishing way up north somewhere. He had been gone for hours by the time I got there. He does it every year. His big Labor Day fishing trip is an annual event." Dr. Androvich snickered.

"What about your own wife. Weren't you scared she might find you out?" asked detective Anderson.

Dr. Androvich gave a haughty response. "Never. I am a doctor. I can get called to the hospital any day, any time of day or night. You get the picture?"

"I see," said Detective Anderson. He stood and walked to the door. He did not feel like shaking the hand of this man who gave him the creeps. "Don't leave town. I may have more questions for you later."

"I'll be right here," said Dr. Androvich. He had a big grin on his face. He clasped his hands behind his head and leaned back in his chair. With one foot, he pushed on his desk to turn his chair around to look out the window. He put his other foot on the window ledge and rocked his chair back and forth. He sighed deeply.

"She was a beautiful woman, and I was her library."

Dr. Androvich stared out the window, thinking about Allesandra Lewis.

CHAPTER 33
THE RED MUSTANG

Friday, August 30, Labor Day Weekend

It was six o'clock in the evening at the Lewises' home.

"Sandra, I'm about ready to go. Jimmy is in the car already. We will be back Tuesday night," James called up the stairs of the big house.

"Fine!" yelled Sandra. She came out of the bedroom and leaned over the top stair railing. "Have a good time." She blew him a kiss, but she didn't mean it. Things were always so tense between them. It was a relief to have him take Jimmy off her hands for a few days. "I have a good book to keep me busy all weekend," she said.

"I'm sure you do," said James begrudgingly. He could hardly get any conversation or attention from her at all these days. She was either gone to the library or she had her nose in a book. He looked up at her and thought, *Beautiful, but a demon for sure.*

Sandra stood still and listened for the car door to shut. Excitement was brewing in her chest. She could feel her heart beating. Then she heard the car drive away. Quickly, she ran her bath water and filled it right up to the overflow. She poured in perfumed oil, tore off her clothes, and slipped in. She relaxed back in the water right up to her chin. She closed her eyes and dreamed of riches and romance.

*****

James was heartbroken. He was feeling completely rejected by Sandra. She didn't want to believe she was having an affair, but he had to find out the truth before he left town. He drove only four miles to a small nearby lake where he thought he could set up camp for just one night and not be seen by anyone else. He pulled off on a barely used dirt road and found a small clearing about fifty feet from the lake. It seemed secluded enough and safe enough to leave Jimmy alone there for as long as was necessary, even if it was all night.

James set up his smallest tent but only unpacked Jimmy's sleeping bag and rolled it out inside. He made a tiny campfire and let Jimmy roast a couple of hotdogs and a few Marshmallows for supper. James ate nothing. He was feeling nervous. He pulled a piece of paper from his pocket and read it and then crumpled it up. Then he smoothed it out and read it again and folded it and put it back in his pocket.

They could be five or five hundred miles away from home, and Jimmy would not know the difference. He did not look retarded, however. He was sixteen this year and six foot tall. His jet-black hair was patchy through the scars on his burnt head. The burn scars on his face did not deter from his good looks. He had a sweet nature and an easy grin. He was just simple—very, very simple. He very rarely said a word. He had one quirk that would work in James's favor tonight. He was afraid of the dark. Jo had instilled that fear in him. He was only following her lead.

As soon as James thought he might be able to get away, he settled Jimmy down in the tent to sleep and promised him he would be just fine until Dad came to bed. Jimmy was too simple to notice there was no sleeping bag set up for Dad. James knew Jimmy would not venture out of the tent on his own because he would be too afraid of the dark to even look out. Jo had taught him that too.

"Don't ever look out the dark windows, Jimmy," she had said to him. "The boogey man lives out there in the dark." She wasn't trying to tease him because she really did believe it herself.

James sat by the fire and stared at it until it completely burned out. He stirred the glowing embers. He peeked in on Jimmy and saw that he was asleep. Then he hopped in his car and drove back to Havana. He drove to the schoolyard and parked where there were no houses. Then he walked the five blocks to his house. It was a big white house, easy to spot, even in the dark. He loved it. He had worked long hours and saved as much as possible until he had enough money to buy it.

For Sandra, he thought. *Funny how everything I did I thought I was doing for her, yet she feels I do nothing for her.*

Sandra and his mother had become enemies while living in the same house, and he wanted Sandra to have her own place to furnish and decorate. She had a lot of energy. Hopefully, that would make her content.

He could feel that nothing he did up to that point had made her happy. He had thought marrying her would make her happy. It did not. He then thought a baby would make her happy. It did not. A second baby? No. A third baby? Absolutely not. She was especially morose after Jo was born.

He didn't want a fourth baby because he thought he couldn't afford another child. He was saving money for the big house, but oddly enough, Sandra seemed to want that one. He was so shocked when she informed him she was pregnant because they barely even had sexual relations. Did the fourth one make her happy? No.

James finally bought the big house and moved his young family of six into it. Did that make her happy? No.

Looking at the house, he saw there were no lights on anywhere and then he saw what he was looking for but hoping not to find. His heart began to race and pound so loud he thought it might burst right out of his chest. Yes, there it was, blatantly parked just a few houses away on his street—a red 1968 convertible Mustang that he knew belonged to Dr. Jackson Androvich. The black top was up.

James glanced at his watch. It was ten thirty. It was a quiet night in a small town. The air was crisp but not cold. The sky was ablaze with twinkling stars. The three quarter moon was giving off plenty of night light. Perfect camping weather. James inched slowly closer to his house, feeling like his body was heavy with two tons of pain. He could barely move. He leaned against the back of his garage, thinking he was out of sight, and debated with himself about what he should do.

"Should I just wait until he comes out and confront him? Should I charge right in there and confront them together? Should I wait until he leaves and confront Sandra alone? Should I wait until he comes out and attack him." He felt like there was a knife in his heart, and it was twisting deeper and deeper with pain.

James wanted to run away, but he didn't. He wanted to put on his boxing gloves and beat the hell out of Dr. Androvich, but he didn't. He wanted to go to his mother's house and get his goose gun and shoot them both. He thought about that for a long time, but he didn't. He wanted to start screaming at the top of his lungs and tell the whole neighborhood what was going on, but he didn't. He waited.

Every minute seemed to drag on excruciatingly. Every minute that went by, James imagined what they were doing in there, in his house. With each passing minute, he was more and more tortured in his spirit.

Then…finally…he heard the back door open. His eyes were adjusted to the dark now, and he plainly saw Dr. Androvich quietly leave his house and walk to his waiting red Mustang.

James froze in a panic-gripped state. He couldn't do any of the things he was thinking about doing. He just stood there and watched until the red Mustang was completely out of sight and hearing.

He took a deep breath and began his slow and torturous walk to the house. He quietly opened the back door. It was never locked. There wasn't even a key for the door. Just as quietly, James closed the door behind him and walked to the bottom of the stairs.

*****

It was only a couple of minutes after Sandra had heard Dr. Androvich leave. She heard a knock on the stairwell wall. Hoping he had second thoughts of leaving and was back for more, she rushed to the upper stair railing and leaned over it.

"Dr. Andro, you're back already?" she called down in her best flirting way.

Standing in the same place where he was the last time he saw her, James looked up and thought, *Even in the dark of night, she is beautiful.* He said, "Yes, Allesandra, I am back," and with his eyes on her, he began deliberately climbing the sixteen stairs to the top.

Sandra was so alarmed when she realized who it was that she almost fell over the bannister. She gasped and backed away into her bedroom and sat down on the bed. She was seized with guilt for the first time in her life. She began thinking of lies that could give her a way out of this predicament.

James stood in the doorway and looked at Sandra. His lower lip began to quiver when he opened his mouth to talk, so it was a full minute before he could get his first word out.

"I...I have something I want to read to you. I have been preparing it for a while because I have suspected you and the good Dr. Androvich for a long time." James turned on the light and looked at Sandra. "Wow," he said. "Pretty sexy outfit you have on there. How come I have never seen it before?"

Sandra had turned white. All the blood drained from her face, and she couldn't speak or move.

James reached into his pant pocket and pulled out a crumpled piece of paper.

Silently, Sandra scooted back onto the bed and pulled her shaking knees up to her chest, wrapping her arms around them. She put her head down on her knees. She didn't have the nerve to look him in the face.

"I know how you love quoting Bible verses to back up your own twisted theology. Well, I found a few that back up my religion. Anyway, it used to be religion. Now I suppose it is just agonizingly twisted theology, just like yours." James smoothed out the paper and began his oration.

"Place me like a seal over your heart," he read. "Like a seal on your arm. For love is as strong as death, its jealousy as enduring as the grave. Love flashes like fire, the brightest kind of flame."[9]

He looked up from the paper and said, "Allesandra Lewis, you are the love of my life. I was a shy, dull man, and you were the love that flashed like fire. The fire I needed to burn through life. You were

---

[9] Song of Solomon 8:6 (NLT)

my little demon in red." He stopped for a few seconds to choke back a sob and regain his composure. "This jealousy is tearing me apart."

Turning back to his paper he said, "Many waters cannot quench love; rivers cannot sweep it away. If one were to give all the wealth of one's house for love, it would be utterly scorned."[10] Tears were dropping onto the paper.

He looked up again. She did not lift her head, so he said, "I will never stop loving you. I have tried so hard, but I can't. The fire of your love burns flaming red in my heart. It can't be quenched." He paused and then turned the paper over.

"If a man is found lying with a married woman," he continued to read, "then both of them shall die, the man who lay with the woman, and the woman; thus you shall purge the evil from Israel.[11] Jealousy makes a man furious, and he will not spare when he takes revenge.[12] God help us."

He looked up, and she was crying with her face in a pillow. He folded the paper and stuffed it back into his pocket. He turned to the door and switched off the light, just as he knew he was switching off his marriage as well, and he walked away. Walked down the stairs, walked out of the house that he had worked so hard for, and walked back to his car.

James headed back to his secret temporary campsite to get Jimmy and head up to Red Lake for the rest of the weekend. The reality of seeing Dr. Androvich coming out of his house had put him in a state of shock. It was a false sense of calm.

The car pulled up to the tent, and the noise awakened Jimmy. He looked around and found himself alone in the dark, and he started to fret. He began to get more agitated and called out.

"Dad! Dad!" he shouted.

James unzipped the tent. "I'm right here, Jimmy."

"Ein dah one dat gotted buuned," Jimmy said.

---

[10] Song of Songs 8:7(NIV)
[11] Deuteronomy 22:22 (https://bible.knowing-jesus.com/topics/Adulterers)
[12] Proverbs 6:34 (ESV)

"Yes," said James. "But you're okay now. Come on with Dad. We have to pack everything up and go to a different place."

"Dad," was Jimmy's only response. He could smile now since his stress was relieved, and he helped James pack up the tent and sleeping bag. They got in the car and headed up to Red Lake.

They didn't get past Owatonna before James's explosive temper took over. Feelings of uncontrollable anger simmered inside. He turned the car around and drove like a madman back to Havana. He pulled into his driveway. The house was still completely dark. He leaped out of the car and yelled a command at Jimmy as if he were just a dog.

"Stay!" He shut the car door and ran to the house, opened the door, and ran up the sixteen stairs two at a time. The bedroom door was open, and Sandra was lying there in bed, sound asleep. Her precious double wedding ring quilt was covering her right up to her neck.

I wonder why that blanket is so special to her? James thought. *Her marriage sure isn't.*

Looking at her so peaceful in sleep while he was so broken in his heart caused a rage to boil up and over and out.

"How could you just go right back to sleep!" he screamed at her and pulled the covers off the bed.

*****

Jimmy would not stay in the car alone. It was dark, and he knew there was a boogey man out there.

"Dad! Dad!" he yelled out. Then he opened the car door and got out and ran to the house as fast as he could. Blackie was on the porch and went right in the house with Jimmy. It was dark in there too, so Jimmy ran to the stairs and called out, "Dad! Dad!"

He looked up the stairwell. It was all dark, but he could hear James and Sandra screaming at each other. Tremendous fear engulfed him. Their fighting always made him tremble. His sweet and simple nature didn't understand hostility. He ran up the stairs as fast as he could. He dashed to his parents' bedroom. It was dark in there too but just light enough from the light of the moon so Jimmy could see both of his parents fighting furiously.

"Dad! Dad!" Jimmy screamed out, adding to their bedlam.

James had his hands around Sandra's neck, and she was pummeling him with all her force. James began laughing at her because she was no match for his strength.

"These hands," James teased, "are a lethal weapon. And I want to squeeze the breath and very life out of you." He pressed her neck, reeling with the torture of betrayal in his soul. She was still able to scream obscenities at him and kick and pound him with all her might.

Jimmy began to pace and wring his hands together. He tried to pull them apart to no avail as the insanity of rage engulfed them.

"No, mine Dad!" he yelled at Sandra. He opened the closet door and saw the fighting knife in the grey scabbard that Dad said would protect from the enemy.

"No, no, Jimmy," he said as he pulled the knife from its cover. He tossed the scabbard to the floor.

"Dad! Dad!" Jimmy shouted as he tried to separate his parents with one hand.

Then, without understanding, Jimmy plunged the knife into his mother's back. Sandra still struggled for thirty seconds before she fainted and fell down on her face. At first James did not realize the situation.

"Sandra," he called to her. She didn't move. "Sandra," he bent down and touched the back of her head. That is when he saw the knife and the bleeding wound.

"Oh my God, Sandra!" he yelled. He pressed her neck with his fingers and found the carotid artery. Her beating heart had already been silenced. "Oh my God, Jimmy!" he yelled.

Shock and horror swept over the room as the man and boy stared down at their lifeless wife and mother lying in blood. James instinctively drew Jimmy back so neither of them stepped in the blood.

In a panic and a shock wave, James grabbed Jimmy and pulled him down the stairs and outside the house, unintentionally leaving Blackie inside. He was completely unaware of the dog's presence.

"What should I do God? This should have never happened. I've got to think this out." James slowly walked to his car, still pulling Jimmy along.

He opened Jimmy's door and said, "Get in the car, Jimmy. Mama is sleeping. We are going fishing." Then, without hurrying or sleeping, he drove to Red Lake.

CHAPTER 34
THE RED AND WHITE QUILT

Wednesday, September 4, Very Early Morning

The sun wasn't up yet, but James was walking back and forth in two bedrooms of the upstairs in his mother's house. He was remembering the happier days when his young family was growing. He still used the smallest bedroom for an office. The second one at one time was a bedroom for all three toddlers, Jessie, Johnny, and Jo.

The large bedroom was his and Sandra's. He glanced at the bed, remembering the many times of pure passion that passed between him and Sandra. He pictured it made up with the red and white double wedding ring quilt on it.

She loved that blanket, he thought. *I know it comforted her when she was upset.* He recalled many times in the winter months, he would happen to find her after supper in the big house in their bedroom sitting in the big stuffed chair, her legs stretched out on the ottoman, with the red and white double wedding ring quilt wrapped around her and her nose in a romance novel.

He sighed. "I guess I failed her. I was not able to meet her expectations of romance, so she had to get it from the books," he said out loud. *Maybe the quilt to her was to her just like Nadahunga is to Jo—a cozy comforter. Maybe they do have something in common after all*, he thought.

James looked into the cute little nursery off to one side, where Jimmy slept until he was two. After that, they moved into the big house just a few blocks away. James felt such pain in his heart, but he kept trying to think of the happier times when the kids were little.

James knew he had a tough day ahead of himself. He knew what had to be done. His mind planned while his feet paced.

Chapter 35

The Red Morning Sun

Finally, a red sun clothed in red clouds was peeking above the horizon. The sky was glowing red. James thought about the old sailors poetic prediction: "Red sky at night, sailors' delight. Red sky at morning, sailors take warning."

He had been a sailor in the navy. He knew if the morning skies are red, it is because clear skies over the horizon to the east permit the sun to light the undersides of moisture-bearing clouds. The saying assumes that more such clouds are coming in from the west.[13] He could now see that for the past twenty years, he had sailed through life without understanding the warning signs.

"What a fool I have been," he said to the early morning sun. "I have not been a very good sailor."

It was early, but he was sure of the things that must be done, and he felt the sooner, the better for all.

He left a note for Clara on the kitchen table.

It read: "Dear Mom, I am going away for a while. Thank you for all that you have done for me over the years. Please watch out for all of your grandchildren. Just a reminder, you have four. Love you, James."

He got in his car and drove up the street to Henrietta's house. Stepping out of his car, he looked at her beautiful flower garden. He picked a daisy and gently knocked on her door. He stepped back and waited.

---

[13] https://en.wikipedia.org/wiki/Red_sky_at_morning

Within a few minutes, Henrietta showed her face at the window of the door. When she saw James, she couldn't get the door open fast enough.

"Oh, James," she grabbed him and hugged him hard. "How terrible everything must be for you. No one knew how to get ahold of you. I am absolutely sick about what happened to Sandra. And Jo, oh my poor little Jo. I know she could not have done such a horrible thing. Please come in."

"Thanks, Henrietta," James felt hesitation but knew he had no choice but to move forward with his plan.

"Are you here to take Jimmy? He is still sleeping. Actually, I was about to get him up and ready for school," said Henrietta.

"Ah, no, not yet. I need a favor though," said James.

"Sit down, James," said Henrietta as she quickly went about the task of making coffee for the two of them. "I will make us some coffee."

James took a deep breath and tried to relax. "That will be great. I really need a little pick-me-up."

"Of course, James, anything. I will do anything to help," she said.

"Could you keep Jimmy for a while?" asked James. "I brought you his clothes from the trip, but they all need washing. I am not able to get back into the house yet, and these are all he has right now.

"Yes, of course, as long as you need me to. And, yes, I will wash his clothes. He is no trouble at all," replied Henrietta. "I have to know. How is my Jo? I tried to see her right away, but I was told she was unable to have visitors yet. They would not give me anymore information than that since I was not family." It felt hurtful because in her heart, she knew Jo was family.

James hung his head and shook it. "No, I have not seen her yet. I am on my way up to the detention center though. I will let you know everything after I see her. I hope you don't mind. I couldn't help myself. I picked this daisy to take to her." James laid it on the table.

"I am so glad you did that." She reached up on a high shelf in the cupboard behind the table and pulled down a little vase. "Here, take this, and pick a few more on the way out." She put a little water in it, then took the daisy from the table and put it in the vase.

The coffee pot began to percolate. Henrietta put two empty cups on the small table and sat down across from James. She put her elbows on the table, folded her hands, bowed her head, and prayed. "Dear God, in all our ways we acknowledge You, and we trust that You will direct our paths. Amen."[14]

They sat in silence for a couple of minutes until the coffee was ready. Henrietta stood up and poured James a cup and then one for herself and sat down. They each poured in a little cream and took a sip. They did not look at each other, Henrietta for fear of breaking down and James for fear of telling her the truth.

When James's cup was empty, he said, "You have been a good friend to all of us for all these years. Twenty-three, twenty-four years?"

"That's close enough," said Henrietta, nodding.

"Well, thanks," said James as he stood up. "I have to get going to Owatonna to see Jo." He picked up the little vase.

"Don't worry about Jimmy." Henrietta was comforting. "He is just fine here. I will take him to and from school for as long as you need me to."

"Goodbye," said James. "You are an angel."

They both stepped out side and Henrietta picked a few more daisies and put them in the vase.

"Goodbye, James," said Henrietta.

---

[14] Proverbs 3:6 (NKJV)

Chapter 36
Evelyn Holyfield

Wednesday, September 4, Early Morning

Those annoying blats from the loudspeaker woke me up. I got up and got dressed and sat on the edge of my cot, waiting for the "step away from the door" command to send me to breakfast. I was really hungry today and was determined to eat all my food no matter what it was.

It wasn't long before the door of my cell opened without warning. The matron who previously hit me with her baton came in. I didn't think I had done anything wrong, but I felt uneasy right away.

"Come with me," she said.

I followed silently like the dumb sheep I had learned to become. I was surprised when she took me to the showers and told me to strip. I did. Then she handed me a bar of soap, put a squirt of shampoo in my other hand, and pointed me to the already running shower.

I gladly stepped up to the lukewarm water and let it pour over me. There was a ledge to set the bar of soap so I could wash my hair first. Then I soaped up, scrubbed up, rinsed off, shut the water off, and stepped out. The matron who had never taken her eyes off me handed me a towel. I dried off, and she handed me a clean uniform. I put it on and looked at the number. It was mine. That felt so good. At least the shower felt good. I wanted to thank her but decided to remain silent in case I said the wrong thing. As for the clean uniform? Twiggy wouldn't like it. Then she handed me a comb and told me to comb my hair. Ah, that felt so good too.

"Follow me," she said.

I did. She took me to the cafeteria and told me to get my breakfast. I picked up my tray and followed her to the table. I was surprised when she sat down across from me. I was starving. It smelled so good. A hard-boiled egg, a piece of dry toast, a sausage link, and an orange. I glanced at the matron who wasn't paying much attention to me while I ate. She had a name tag above her left breast pocket on her uniform.

Evelyn Holyfield, I read it and said it to myself as I tore into my food and ate every bite. *And she is working in an unholy field*, I thought.

I felt gratitude to her for the shower and the edible food. It is amazing how a person appreciates the littlest thing when one has been deprived.

After breakfast, Evelyn Holyfield told me to follow her again. She took me to a large room that looked like a sitting room.

She pointed to a table and said, "Sit there and wait. You are going to be arraigned today for the murder of Allesandra Lewis. Your lawyer will be here soon to let you know what is expected of you while you are before the judge. Good luck." She walked out and shut the door.

Good luck? She actually wished me good luck, I thought. *Maybe she is human after all, with an ever so slight touch of compassion.* I wasn't very sure what arraignment meant, but I was prepared to speak the truth and nothing but the truth, so help me God. Now that I could remember.

I waited for Jacob Sanders.

*****

James arrived at the detention center just at eight in the morning. He checked in and thankfully found his name was on the list of allowed visitors for Jo Lewis. In fact, his was the only name on the list other than Dr. Westfield and Jacob Sanders.

A prison officer signed in James and then searched him. "Ah, sorry, sir, but you can't take that in there," he said, pointing to the vase.

"Could I just take the flowers and not the vase?" asked James as he pulled the four daisies out and tossed the vase in the wastebasket.

"All right," said the officer, relenting.

James was then led through two separate locked-barred doors. The officer pointed to a door that said "Visitors' Room" on the plaque.

"Please go in there, Mr. Lewis. Your daughter is already in there waiting for her lawyer this morning."

"Thank you," said James. He walked across the lobby and opened the door. Once he stepped in, the officer stepped in behind him and stood beside the door.

*****

I was so surprised when the door opened, and instead of Jacob, there was my dad, at last.

"Jo!" he called to me with his arms wide open.

"Dad!" I screamed out in pure joy. I leaped up and ran to him. We hugged so hard and just cried for a few minutes. Neither of us could speak.

"Please sit at the table," said the officer.

We sat quickly. I was learning to do as I was told behind bars.

Dad handed me the flowers.

"Henrietta?" I asked, smiling. They had become my favorite flower.

"Yes," said Dad. "She tried to get in here to see you but was told no since she was not family."

"Dad, what happened?" I asked. He didn't respond but just shook his head. "It is unbelievable what happened to Mother. I am so sorry," I whispered. I didn't want to incriminate him just in case he did it, so I was afraid to speak any details.

He put his hands on the table, and I put mine in his without letting go of the daises.

"She was a very beautiful woman, that mother of yours. She had a popular saying that she loved to use on you teenagers whenever you made a mistake. It keeps going through my mind. 'You made your bed, now you lie in it.' I think she is speaking to me even after death."

"What are you talking about, Dad? What happened? Did you go to Red Lake?" I asked.

"Yes, we did," he responded.

"That's a relief." I sighed deeply. Dad was in a mood I had never seen. I didn't know what to make of it. I just couldn't read him.

"How are you doing in here, Jo?" he asked. "I am so sorry you are here."

"Well, it has been stressful, to say the least," I said. "Dad," I whispered. "You know I didn't kill Mother, don't you?"

"Yes, Jo, I know you could never have done anything like that. You have nothing to worry about. Trust me," he said quietly.

"Why, do you know something?" I wanted details. My future was at stake here.

"I know who did it, Jo," he whispered. "You will find out very soon. I am on my way to the police station, but I needed to see you first and make sure you were all right. I am so sorry you got messed up in this."

"You have one minute left, Mr. Lewis. Please say your goodbyes," announced the officer on guard.

We stood. We hugged. We cried. We said goodbye, but I never let go of the daises.

CHAPTER 37
THE RED BRICK BUILDING

James had prayed for guidance from the God of heaven and earth. His mind was set on what he knew he must do. He drove to the police station in downtown Owatonna. He parked his car a few blocks away and set his eyes on the red brick building down the block that was the police station. He did not walk fast, and he did not walk slowly. He walked with determination. Once inside, he asked for Detective Anderson.

"Okay, Mr. Lewis," said the receptionist. "Detective Anderson is in the building. Please step into that vacant office over there and have a seat. I will let him know you want to see him."

James walked in to the office and sat down.

It wasn't long before he saw Detective Anderson through the glass partition, speaking with the receptionist. The detective looked over at James and nodded at him. James nodded back.

James prayed again. "Help me, God, to not waver in this."

The detective entered the office and closed the door. "Good morning, Mr. Lewis," he began. "I am just preparing to go to the courthouse where they will be bringing your daughter over for arraignment. Her lawyer, Jacob Sanders, will be with her there. I am glad to see you. You can go with me for support for Jo. Actually, I was just going to call you to meet me there."

James was silent, unable to speak the words he came to say.

"I read your deposition, and I have questioned Dr. Androvich. The prosecution still has their eyes on Jo," he continued. "They feel the case is rock solid. I am so sorry, Mr. Lewis."

James fidgeted in his chair and took out his handkerchief and wiped his sweating brow. Finally, the courage he was waiting for surged into his thirsty soul.

"Ah…I…er…" James paused and cleared his throat. "Detective Anderson." James stood up.

The detective looked James squarely in the eyes and said, "Yes?"

"I came here to tell you Jo did not murder her mother. You were right when you said it looks like a domestic." He paused and took a deep breath.

"You have my attention," said Detective Anderson.

"I did not leave town early that evening. I took Jimmy to a close campsite, left him there, and, well after dark, went back to Havana. I was suspecting my wife of an affair as I said before, so I intended to catch them," said James.

"Stop right there, Mr. Lewis, and have a seat please," said the detective.

James sat down and sighed. He felt calmer now and was quite sure of his resolve.

"You have the right to remain silent and refuse to answer questions," said Detective Anderson. "Anything you say may be used against you in a court of law. You have the right to consult an attorney before speaking to the police and to have an attorney present during questioning now or in the future. If you cannot afford an attorney, one will be appointed for you before any questioning, if you wish. If you decide to answer questions now without an attorney present, you will still have the right to stop answering at any time until you talk to an attorney.[15] Knowing and understanding your rights as I have explained them to you, are you willing to continue without an attorney present?"

"Yes," said James without faltering. "Just as I suspected, Dr. Androvich's car was on my street. I stood outside, watched my house, and waited for him to leave. As soon as his car was out of sight, I went in the house. I found Sandra upstairs. We argued. We fought physically. I was in a rage. I stabbed her right in the back. I didn't

---

[15] https://en.wikipedia.org/wiki/Miranda_warning

mean to kill her. I only wanted to threaten her, to scare her straight. She fell to the floor. When I realized she was dead, I left. I went back to the campsite I gathered up the camping stuff and Jimmy and drove up to Red Lake."

Detective Anderson took a deep breath and nodded his head. James put out his hands. Slowly and deliberately Detective Anderson took out his handcuffs, grabbed James's wrist, and pulled him up to stand. He turned him around and cuffed him behind his back.

Chapter 38
Free at Last

I watched Dad leave. He left me standing there in complete wonderment. I wasn't sure what to think.

"Please sit at the table, Jo. Your lawyer will be here soon," said the prison officer.

Time was going by, and it seemed endless waiting. I held the daises in my hand. I felt like they were a sign from an angel that everything was going to be all right. I remembered that daisies never lie. They always say I love you.

I was thinking with a mind of anticipation. Instead of thinking about the past, I thought about the future. "If Dad knows who did it, I will be set free soon. That means I can get back to work at Salet's. Robert will be coming home in the spring, and we can get married. Life is good," I said to myself.

I could dream about Robert for hours on end. He is the only boy I ever loved. I am pretty sure I am the only girl he ever loved. The thoughts made me smile and relax. Then I began feeling a little bolder.

"Excuse me sir," I asked the officer. "Could you tell me what time it is?"

"Sure," he said and glanced at his watch. "It is eleven o'clock."

Oh boy, I thought. *I think I have been here over three hours.*

Just then, the door opened. Jacob Sanders walked in with a big smile on his face. Evelyn Holyfield was right behind him with some folded clothes.

"Good news, Jo. Are you ready for some good news?" he asked.

"Yes, yes, yes," I said.

He took a deep breath and said, "I have good news, but along with that, I have bad news."

"Okay, just tell me," I was already impatient.

"You are free to go," he said. He took another deep breath and decided he could not tell me about my dad yet. He still feared for my mental health.

"And?" I asked.

"And you will have to follow Officer Holyfield back to your cell one last time to change your clothes and get your personal belongings. The bad news is you will be missing lunch here today." He laughed.

I sang the doxology for the joy that welled up within. "Praise God, from Whom all blessings flow; Praise Him, all creatures here below; Praise Him above, ye heavenly host; Praise Father, Son, and Holy Ghost.[16] Amen."

*****

I got dressed in my street clothes. There were no personal belongings in my cell. I looked up at the barred window. Even though the sunshine had moved on, I knew it was shining outside, and I felt shiny on the inside from the Son.

I followed Evelyn one last time to the jailhouse foyer where I retrieved my promise ring. I gladly slipped it onto my waiting ring finger. I took a deep breath and felt whole again. Jacob was waiting there for me.

"Jo," he said. "I will be taking you over to the police station. We will have a follow-up meeting there, and I believe your neighbor, Henrietta Bjornevik, has been called to pick you up from there. I hope that is okay with you."

"Sounds wonderful," I said. But I had yet to know who really did end my mother's life. I didn't ask questions because I was afraid of the truth.

---

[16] http://www.cyberhymnal.org/htm/p/r/praisegf.htm

Chapter 39
Daddy, Don't Sing

I loved hearing the barred gates close and lock behind me as I stepped out into freedom. I stepped out into the sunshine and thanked God that prison was behind me forever.

Just as he said, Jacob drove me to the police station. Once we arrived, I put my hand on the door handle to open my side of the car. Jacob reached over and put his hand on my left wrist.

"Wait a minute, Jo," he said. He had decided to just blurt it out like one would tear off a Band-Aid. "I do have bad news, and I want to tell you before we go in. Your father has confessed to and been arrested for the murder of your mother." He looked at me and waited for a response.

I nodded my head a bit. I took a deep breath and blew out all of my breath and did it again to clear my emotions. It was as if I was trying not to throw up, only this time, I was trying not to cry. I was so sick of crying.

"I did suspect it at first, but I just couldn't make myself believe it," I said calmly. I looked at the daisies in my hand.

"All right then. Are you okay to go in and face him?" he said.

"I think I am," I said, although feeling very, very sad, way down in the heart of my soul.

"Okay, Jo, let's go," said Jacob, sounding encouraging.

I smiled just a little. "That is something my dad would say," I said.

"We will see what we can do to help him," said Jacob.

I got out of the car and went into the police station with Jacob. I waited while he talked with the receptionist. We were directed to a room where Dad was already there. I walked in, and he stood to hug me. But he was cuffed behind his back, so I was the one who did the hugging. We didn't say anything at all. We didn't need to.

Then I noticed Henrietta was there already too. I ran to her even though she was only a few steps away from me. She hugged me and patted my hair. I could tell she had been crying.

"We will get through this together, Jo," she assured me.

Detective Anderson must have thought Dad was not a threat anymore because he got up and uncuffed Dad's hands, turned him around, and recuffed him in the front.

We all sat at the table.

"I have a lot of things to sort out yet," said Dad. "But a few decisions have been made already. "Jo, Henrietta has wholeheartedly agreed to take over the care of Jimmy."

"He's no trouble at all," said Henrietta.

"I will be making her legal guardian," Dad continued. "Jessie and Johnny refuse to speak to me, so if you are willing and able, Jo, I am asking you to be the executor of my estate. I am giving you complete power of attorney over all my finances. We can work out all the details after the funeral."

"The funeral," I sighed. "That never crossed my mind." I pictured my mother, Allesandra Lewis, dressed in her favorite store-bought red dress, lying in a casket with a huge spray of bright red flowers decorating her death.

"Jessie has agreed to come down from Minneapolis and take care of all the arrangements. I will be allowed to attend under police custody, of course. I hope you can work with her on that since you will be holding the checkbook." He was not smiling, but he was very matter-of-fact.

"Yes, Dad," I said. "Don't worry."

"Johnny has agreed to look after your grandmother. He will come for the funeral and be her escort," said Dad. "I can't think of anything else at this moment."

"Okay then," broke in Detective Anderson. "Come with me now, Mr. Lewis."

We all stood up. Dad came over to me, and we were face to face.

"Jo," he said, sniffing back his tears. "It was an accident. I know it doesn't look like it, but I really loved your mother no matter what."

"I know you did, Dad," I said. I put the daisies in his hand.

"The daisies never lie. They always say I love you." I could barely speak because I was trembling.

Even with his handcuffs on, he started a little pantomime boxing at me, and I boxed his fists back.

"Take care of things, Jo Lewis, my little fighter," he said. "I am counting on you."

I thought that, up to this time, I had cried enough tears to fill a river and could never cry again. But I was wrong. I burst out sobbing.

"Daddy, don't sing such a goodah song!"

Dad walked away but turned back one last time and said, "Don't worry, Shiny. I know that my Redeemer lives, and that in the end, he will stand upon the earth."[17]

The End

---

[17] Job 19:25 (NIV)

About the Author

Jane Pecora's passion for creative writing began in childhood. She has written, directed, and produced nine faith-filled family musicals for her own company, Promise Theatre, in Buffalo, New York. Jane writes personalized wedding songs and Christian worship choruses. Because of her love for Bible study, she graduated from Elim Bible Institute in 2008 and is a speaker at women's events. Her love of storytelling led her to write *Red: The Color of Murder*, which is based in her hometown state, Minnesota. Jane is also a registered nurse. She has seven children. Two were adopted, and two are stepchildren. Jane and her husband, Ed, now divide their time between Buffalo and Florida.